Suicidal Gods

BY C.M. CHAPMAN

Suicidal Gods

BY C.M. CHAPMAN

For information contact:
Unsolicited Press
Portland, Oregon
www.unsolicitedpress.com
orders@unsolicitedpress.com
619-354-8005

Cover Design: Brigid Hokana
Editor: Jay Kristensen Jr.

ISBN: 978-1-950730-13-1

I AM OVERWHELMED by the number of people I'd like to thank for setting me off on this journey. Sincerest thanks to Linda Bowers who helped make it all possible from the beginning and for her supportive and loving kindness through the years. Many thanks to my friends, J.F. Rote and George Lies, who both played significant roles in reintroducing me to the writing life. And, of course, to the wonderful, enlightening, and supportive MFA mentors and friends along the way, Jessie van Eerden, Eric Waggoner, Carter Sickles, Crystal Wilkinson, Richard Schmitt, and Marie Manilla, who all helped me to become myself on the page. For their support and encouragement, deep appreciation goes to Devon McNamara, Doug van Gundy, and my MFA friend, Tim Moraca, who actually read this book to his new bride on their honeymoon trip. A big thanks to one of my earliest readers, Dana Johnson, and endless gratitude to my parents for reading aloud to me as a child. It all means so much to me. There are many more of you out there. Thank you all.

An earlier version of "Inky-do" was published as "Inky-Do: An Appalachian Tall Tale" in *Dark Mountain*, Issue #7.

An earlier version of "How to Get Away from the World" was published in the Spring 2015 issue of *Cheat River Review*.

"The Eighth Angel" was originally published in the Fall 2015 issue of *Bird's Thumb*.

"Blood" was originally published in the Fall 2015 issue of *Kentucky Review*.

"The Desolation Toad" was originally published in the Fall 2015 issue of *Rose Red Review*.

"Bones" was originally published in the Winter 2016 issue of *Limestone*.

"Report on the Strange Case of Lt. Henry Harper" was originally published in *Floyd County Moonshine*, Issue 8.2, Fall 2016.

"The Moth in the Stair" was originally published in the Winter 2017 issue of *Still: The Journal*.

"Signs" was originally published in *Unlikely Stories*, October 2017.

*For Sherry, without whose love, trust, and endless patience
I could never have found Dogleg Bend.*

Stories

The Desolation Toad

CORALINE WAS DESTINED to be the last. Her mama, Emma Walker, took to bed immediately after the difficult birth, where she grew weaker and frailer as the days passed. She was laid to rest in the Walker family cemetery shortly after her daughter's first birthday. Coraline remembered nothing about her.

Everything she knew about Mama had come from Granny Mag. After their mother died, it was Granny Mag who took care of Coraline and her two older brothers, William and Nathan, moving into their cabin on the warm side of Spenser Mountain, several miles south of where the Dogleg Bend Trading Post sat along the river.

Papa walked the line most every morning, even Sunday, checking his traps from the day before. He didn't have many, so he was choosy about his spots, and his favorites were spread out over a half day's walk. Every day, Papa traipsed into the misty hills with his hunting rifle, Coraline watching from the loft window as the West Virginia morning swallowed him up. He always gave her a kiss and whispered, "My little dog-flower," before he surrendered himself to the mist. Granny Mag, having been named after the magnolia blossom herself, said it was because she was as pretty as the pink flowers on the dogwood.

"He sees your mama in you. You're his only baby girl."

By this time, Coraline knew about her other sisters. Emily had died of fever before she turned four, and Margaret hadn't lived long at all.

"They was both sickly youngins right from the start," said Granny Mag, tying some fox fur to a charm bag. "That's the way it is sometimes, child. I seen it over and over." She reached out and tousled Coraline's hair. "Not you, though. We always knowed you was special, that you was a special *girl*."

Granny Mag smiled when she said things like that, the kind of smile that burrowed deep into Coraline's eyes until she could feel it digging into her heart.

Coraline didn't feel very girly. With two older brothers, she'd grown up from the dirt like a little tree, poking her branches into just about anything. Granny Mag was always yelling at her to get her hands off some living thing, especially toads.

"Coraline," said Granny one day, in the high pitch that meant she was tired of repeating herself, "you best quit handling those toads. Heaven help ya if you ever got aholda the desolation toad—then you'd have some trouble!"

"The des…"

"The word's des-o-la-tion, girl."

"What's a des-olation toad?"

"Never you mind," said Granny Mag. "That's for granny women to know, not little girls."

"Is it pretty like that one?"

"Only you, Coraline, could find a toad pretty. No, now you just stop handling toads once and for all."

"But Granny—"

"But nothing, Coraline. You're six years old. You mind your Granny."

Even Papa obeyed Granny Mag when she said to mind.

"Yes'm."

Desolation. It sounded like a preacher word. Coraline mulled it over, turned it in the soil to see if anything would grow from it. But nothing did.

FOR A FEW weeks in the sudden spring of Coraline's eighth year, a spectral scream echoed through the dark, across Spenser Mountain. The boys all strutted with excitement. The fathers paced in vigilance, their eyes seeking the hand of fate. Papa's traps went untended, and he carried his rifle with him everywhere. Several hunting parties ventured into the hills, but the cat was a ghost, crying, untouchable, always from the other side.

Danger, though, could no more stop Granny Mag than a stiff breeze, and when word came that Jenny Smith was in the throes of childbirth, she readied herself for the walk down the mountain.

"Coraline, your Papa and brothers will be back soon. You are not to move from this cabin, you hear?"

"Yes'm."

Inside, she played with the ragdoll Granny had made, but eventually, Coraline could hold it in no longer. She had to use the privy. Peeking side to side, she slipped out the door, crossing the yard to the gray outhouse. She knew that the snake carved into the top of the door was Granny Mag's doing, but she could never quite figure out why the old shack had a little chimney on top. When she finished, she hurried back to the weathered porch and lingered, looking across the open landscape in front of the cabin: fields of yellow, white, and green pushing upward as if to catch the very mountains around it. She scanned the distance for some sight of her father and brothers coming home to free her from her imprisonment, but there was no movement in the meadow. All was still.

It occurred to her that she had been outside for a while and everything was normal. Everything felt safe, and soon, she was playing in the dirt, snatching young beetles and watching their legs jig. Not long after, the old, wild grapevine just inside the wood line seemed safe enough too. She crossed into the cool world of bark and leaf.

Coraline refused to swing out from the flat rock like William and Nathan did. It was too high for her, but since she wanted the biggest swing possible, she ran straight toward the hanging vine at full speed. She leaped for it and grabbed hold, her feet flying out in front of her even before the bark under her hands slipped. Her head snapped downward, bouncing off of the leaf mold on the forest floor with a soft thud. She felt the jolt: her head hummed like a bee, then roared like a train coming on fast.

She woke to the sight of branches and blue sky, the sound of spring birds, and her brothers' voices, coming closer, calling her name.

Propping herself on one elbow, she looked around. A movement from a few feet above pulled her attention to the flat rock, and there lay the cat. Tawny perfection—beautiful Death—gazed down upon Coraline.

In mere seconds, this face would be permanently etched in her memory. The seemingly random white marks around its eyes, the black around its mouth, the wide nose that Coraline could have laid her hand on and never touched the silver-green eyes that peered through her like she thought only Granny Mag could. The mountain lion's back legs were hunched, ready for action, but the upper half of its body was sprawled across the rock, right leg hanging loose over the side. And its expression: later in life, she would only be able to call it bemused.

The bull rope of a tail twitched and swished, cutting the air. Muscles rippled under loose flesh as it patted its massive paw against the side of the rock, bobbing its head toward her, like it was telling her to do something. Of course, she could do nothing. She hadn't moved a muscle, paralyzed on one elbow, becoming more and more aware of her brothers getting closer, unable to shout a warning.

The cat rose with a languid motion. It looked once more at Coraline and padded away with a softer step than should be expected of a hundred-twenty-pound creature. Her brothers crashed through the forest line as it passed out of sight.

Her oldest brother, Will, screamed, "It's the cat!" and ran back to the house to grab the rifles. He and Nathan pursued it into the hills. Later, Granny Mag pursued *him* with a switch. She was none too happy that the boys hunted the animal that had spared her granddaughter's life. "Don't you know a spirit blessing by now?" she hollered, as Will dodged behind the rocking chair. "Ain't you never listened to nothin I said?"

Cornered, William produced a claw they'd found embedded in a tree the cat had scratched. Granny Mag took it and spared him the switch.

"But I was gonna keep that as a good luck charm!" William cried. Granny Mag gave him her coldest stare and there was no arguing with that. His luck, though, had indeed run out. Papa had a thing or two to say to him about chasing the animal without seeing to his little sister first. Those lessons were imparted between lashes of the belt. When he finished, he called for Coraline.

"You know how lucky you are?" asked Papa.

Coraline nodded, looking at the floor.

"I'm going to guess that the scare learned ya more than my belt ever could."

"Yes, Papa."

"Not a person on this mountain would ever disobey your granny. She's a wise woman. She don't say things just to say 'em. You remember that."

"I know, Papa. I'm sorry."

That night, she awoke to the mountain lion in her bed, bobbing its head and pawing at her with its massive clawed foot as if prodding her to action. She was not afraid, and when the cat stood, she followed it—though she wasn't sure, once outside, how she got there. The cat led her up the dirt road toward the cabin where Granny Mag had lived before moving in with them. It jumped onto the front porch and sprawled there. As she approached, it purred. She reached out for it and then found herself back in her bed. Later, she told Granny Mag about the dream and got one of those looks.

Granny Mag didn't say anything to her for three days, but on the second day, she approached Coraline and, without a word, slipped a knotted necklace over her head. Dangling from the leather, the cat's claw rested on her chest. From that day forward, she was Granny Mag's apprentice.

Over the next years, as word of Coraline's dreams spread across Spenser Mountain, it became common knowledge that she had received her gift of Sight from the catamount. Later in life, Granny Cora sometimes wondered if it was the bump on the head that brought about that particular gift, and the cat was just amused to see it happen.

CORALINE PRESIDED OVER her first birth by the age of sixteen, long before she was to have any children of her own. She learned to make tinctures of mullein for Della Harper's asthma and infusions of licorice, coltsfoot, and marshmallow root for when the cough would spread across the mountain. She learned to recognize all the herbs and mushrooms before Granny Mag ever started teaching her charm-making.

In the winter of her twentieth year, Papa slipped on a loose stone while checking traps and tumbled into a steep ravine. Coraline and her brothers laid him to rest beside their mother.

At twenty-two, nature would wait no more and presented her with a tall, bright-eyed young man named James Milton. She met him when he came to ask for medicine for his ailing father. The air between them burned hot from the beginning, but Coraline was slow to reciprocate his feelings.

"A granny woman ain't no nun," said Granny Mag, and that was that. Coraline was soon married, and within a few years, gave birth to two boys, Jacob and Daniel. She and James shared the duties of the house, farm and domestic, and as long as she had an infant, Granny Mag let her tend to her own family. Over time, though, Granny Mag watched the boys more and more, while Cora took the walk to deliver the medicine, the charm, or the baby. Jacob was seven when Granny Mag took ill for the last time.

At thirty years old, Coraline knew everything Granny Mag had to teach her, except for the one thing she'd always meant to ask. Granny Mag's eyes opened wide before she told her the last, dark truth.

SOME FIFTY YEARS after her encounter with the catamount and five years after her beloved James was killed by a life of hard work, Granny Cora knew every inch of the mountain. She knew the secret hollow where the ginseng grew like dandelions, the spot at the top of the mountain where the wind wouldn't blow. She knew every spring and stream as if it were her own heart or an artery in her body that flowed outside of her. She lived in deep awareness of the life around her, filled with signs and portents and responsibility.

Now that her grandchildren were coming of age, she moved to the cabin where Granny Mag had spent her last fifteen years. From there, she intended to give herself completely to the mountain and its residents for whatever time she had left.

With her face shrinking like a dried sponge and knees aching like a broken heart, she set out every morning with her walking stick to gather supplies or call on patients. During her life, she had seen many children into the world, including her own grandchildren, but none of them seemed to have the Sight— no dreamers or truth-speakers among them by all appearances—and she was starting to fear that she might be the last granny woman on Spenser Mountain. While she clung to some hope for Jacob's youngest daughter, Amelia, there had been no indication of anything unusual, and the girl was near fourteen. Still, she kept looking for the signs, and taught the girl much of the traditional medicine.

Her eldest, Jacob, hadn't been pleased about her move to the cabin.

"I don't like you being all the way up there by yourself, Ma."

"Quit your worrying, Jacob, I'm fine."

"Takes me a half hour to get up there on foot. You shouldn't be so far."

"So ride your mule then. It's easier to make my rounds from up there. I'll hear no more of it."

He had no choice. Cora was the highest authority on the mountain.

"Ma," he said once, "even old Daniel Webster couldn't win an argument with you. I bet Grover Cleveland couldn't get his way if your mind was set agin it."

Family sometimes pulled her from her center. It had always been that way. Living in Granny Mag's old place, Cora resonated completely with the life around her. The sounds of the mountain were a constant language that she heard more easily when centered in the quiet. Here she was sharpest and most aware.

So, when the summer storm split the night, she sat breathless and wide-eyed, listening as the curtain ripped from in front of the other world.

SHE FOUND THE spot within an hour, just above the hollow where her family lived. The lightning had ripped a black birch in half. The tree was completely burnt, as was a circle some thirty feet wide around it. And there, at the base of charcoal which used to be a beautiful birch, something sat.

It was unmistakably a toad, but freakishly large, nearly eight inches long and six inches wide and therefore slow to register in Cora's mind. Further complicating her comprehension of the creature was the fact that it was predominantly black, with dark brown highlights along its lumpy skin. The colors blended into the burnt, black, and muddy space around it.

In that moment, she knew what it was.

"Only us grannies know about the desolation toad," Granny Mag had said on her deathbed. Cora hadn't been able to tell which was causing her more pain, the dying or the telling. "Just hope you never see one, child. It's said the gaze of the toad brings ruin onto you and yourn. I mean *total* ruin, y'hear? I heard it told Jamestown fell to the gaze of the toad."

Granny Mag looked away.

"Oh! I wish you hadn't asked about that, wish you didn't remember that at all. It's a bad omen Coraline, a bad omen."

"Is there nothing to be done for it?"

"Nothing," said Granny Mag, appearing to drift away on a pool of sorrow. "I met a granny woman once passing through here who warned me it was near. She survived seeing the thing, but couldn't do nothing to stop the tragedy that followed. That was just before the cholera hit up north. I forget how many years back. She was heading to North Carolina, hoping the rest of her family wouldn't be dead when she got there."

"I remember hearing about the cholera, Granny. Little more'n six years ago, I reckon."

"Well Coraline, you never heard about nothing past the outbreak. Never heard about how it wiped out two entire families, entire bloodlines. The ones not taken by disease or the Brothers War died in all manner. She told me. Pray the spirits you never see one girl." Cora promised she would.

But now, here was the toad. On *her* mountain. So close to her own kin. Granny Cora clutched the lion claw that rested on her chest.

Something had to be done. This could not happen. Not if she could help it. Despair covered her like carnivorous ivy. For a moment, she considered killing the thing, picking up the largest rock she could find and smashing it beyond recognition. Immediately, though, she remembered Granny Mag chasing William with a switch for not respecting the magic.

It sat motionless, staring at her with its haughty, disapproving frown, its brown eye sockets bugging out of its black head, a blinking, winking freak of oblivion.

"You have to take the bad with the good," Granny Mag would have said. Even with this knowledge, Cora could not let it roam free, so close to gazing on her family. She pulled the burlap sack from where she kept it tied to her walking stick and approached the creature. The toad did not attempt to escape as she shoved it in the sack with trembling hands. Her charms would have to protect her. She would hide it away, where it couldn't gaze on anyone, and ask the spirits what to do.

AT HOME, CORA found an apple crate, put the Desolation Toad inside, and covered it with heavy boards and stones. She surrounded the box with every talisman and bit of mountain magic she possessed, praying and chanting all through the day and night for the assistance of the spirits.

Near dawn, she saw Granny Mag in her mind, as she often did when she prayed.

"It is more powerful than you Coraline, more powerful than the mountain, the earth. You must respect the toad's purpose. You must let go."

"Is there nothing to do? Nothing?" Cora was pleading.

"Might as well try to strike the moon from the sky, girl. The thing must serve its purpose. If you would hope to change its course, then stand in a willow circle, say the words, and beg the toad for mercy. But I'll warn you that mercy is not the toad's disposition. It is not the creature's nature to leave until its work is done, no matter how long it takes."

Cora had to try. She had no choice. Her duty was to her family and all the families on and around Spenser Mountain, to all those babies she brought into the world.

The willow she kept for medicinal purposes wouldn't do. It would require a trip down the mountain to find the long flexible shoots she would need to fashion a proper circle. She was exhausted, but set out immediately, dragging her old frame down to the closest willow she knew, and then back up the mountain, loaded with a burlap sack full of long, young willow shoots.

As she cleared the last crest and passed into view of the cabin, pain pinched her chest. Jacob stood there, working on the old out-building that once housed the wood pile. She panicked, but had no breath to yell at him. Jacob saw her and waved.

"Howdy, Ma," he called out. He pointed with his thumb over his shoulder at the mule behind him. "I brought ol' Jerry up here for ya. Thought I'd turn this into a little stable over here."

Maybe it's alright, she thought. Maybe he didn't see.

"Jacob," she finally caught her breath to say. "I don't need a mule."

"Aw, Ma, Jerry's a good mule. He done his part. He needs a break. Carrying you up and down and around this mountain won't be a thing to him. It'll be the good life."

"Jacob—" she started.

"I won't hear any more of it, Ma. Honestly! If you want to stay up here, then you take ol' Jerry, here. That's it. Granny or not."

"Alright, build yer stable, but stay out of the house. I got granny goings on in there."

"You know I don't pry, Ma," he paused. "But I poked my head in there looking for ya and I hafta ask, where in blazes did you ever find a *toad* that *big*? That's a prize-winner there, for sure."

She dropped her bag, ran for the rickety wooden step to the porch and through the ill-fit door. The apple crate sat undisturbed, covered by the heavy stones and boards. The toad squatted atop the crate, partially covering one of her pitiful charms.

It was already too late.

ODDLY, JACOB WAS not the first to die. Her grand-nephew, Lucas, drowned that very afternoon in the river, high and powerful from the rain the night before.

Cora didn't know this when she wove her willow circle, stood in it, and said the words, when she begged the toad for mercy with all her humility and an honest account of the good people of Spenser Mountain. The toad, placed in the circle before her, did not move, did not attempt to escape. It gazed. At what, she could not tell.

Two days later, Jacob was killed when a winch chain snapped at the mill in Dogleg Bend. Over the next several months, misfortunes fell one after another: a devastating fire, a suicide, a wagon accident, sickness, even a drunken murder. Eventually, Calvin and Amelia, her grandchildren, were her only last living relatives. She had sent them closer to town, to stay with a young family she had helped in the past. She didn't want to risk them seeing the toad, who for all this time sat in her cabin, atop the apple crate, surrounded by impotent charms. Magic could not stop desolation.

After each funeral, she returned to the cabin and asked if it was enough now, but the toad only persisted in its implacable frown. Granny Mag had said there was no fighting it and Cora knew, at her core, that magical beings must be respected. She believed it until the day they buried her grandson.

It rained. And the preacher, a young firebrand, new to the area, said, "There shall not be found among you any one that maketh his son or his daughter to pass through the fire, or that useth divination, or an observer of times, or an enchanter, or a *witch*." He looked at Cora. "Only through the heart of our Lord and Savior Jesus Christ will we be saved."

Only her beloved Amelia remained.

It sat still as death on the crate when she returned to the cabin. The thought of the family's utter extinction, the thought of Amelia dying next, fueled her simmering rage as she turned on the toad. "I paid you your respect. But now, I'm beginning not to respect you so much." Her eyes burned almost as hotly as her cheeks. "Oblivion is easy, you cursed toad. It's the living that's hard!"

The toad winked at her.

She shrieked and grabbed her father's old hunting rifle which leaned against the wall. "Well, if you love desolation so much!" She shot it between its bulging eyes, splattering otherworldly toad all over the walls and ceiling of the cabin, then dropped to her knees and apologized to Jesus.

GRANNY CORA DIED after a series of three heart attacks that began a week later.

During the first, her Sight opened to a vision of her granddaughter, with the mountain lion looking over her from the flat rock of her youth. She believed now that the girl would survive.

The vision moved on in the way of dreams, fogging, shifting, lurching, and she saw Amelia, now grown with a husband and three children, living on the mountain, taking care of the family land. Amelia wasn't a granny woman, but Cora saw her, in the vision, occasionally walking up the mountain path to her granny's cabin, smiling bittersweet as she remembered the past.

She awoke on her back, on the cabin floor, at peace. She could die now, she thought, sacrifice herself and pay the toad's final price.

The second heart attack occurred two days later, harder and more sudden than the first. It began in darkness, until a pinprick of light began to grow, stretching out in front of her. She looked upon a field, or at least what used to be a field, in the old world somewhere, she thought. Now, it was burnt and blighted. Huge scars were dug across the landscape and tangles of sharp metal thorns decorated the scars. A cloud of yellow wind swept across the landscape like the sulfurous fumes of Hell. She saw a boy on his knees, propping himself on a bulky rifle, choking to death in that poisonous air and, in that instant, knew it was her great-grandson under that metal hat. He was the last, taken in some future war. The bloodline was dead. Cora awoke wishing she was. The left side of her body would not move, but she managed to drag herself to Granny Mag's old rocker and pull herself into it.

She had not moved when the third, and final, heart attack struck a few hours later.

The Sight opened to her once more and she was helpless to refuse it. Again, the vision thrust her into a blasted, pitted land, with huge scars and clouds of death floating through the air. As her vision pulled her back and away from the land, she saw great, nightmarish, metal beasts eating and vomiting the earth and, for as far as she could see in that direction, all was devastation. It looked like the end of the world and the horror of understanding soon dawned upon her.

This plateau of ruin was all that was left of Spenser Mountain, her mountain. They were all gone, the mountain spirits, the animals, the streams, the trees, all life's creation, swallowed into some dark hole. Everything she loved, gone.

Then, her vision flew her up and away from the rutted destruction on her way to the other world, and below her, she saw a tiny speck in the middle of the ruin that seemed more densely black with a gravity all its own. Even from high up here, she knew what it was. Because only a granny can truly understand desolation.

Signs

KERMIT HAMRICK ARRIVED home shortly after six to find Betty asleep on the couch, dressed in the same t-shirt and sweats she wore yesterday. He let the door close sharply. She didn't stir. On the television, an infomercial expounded the secrets of youth.

Checking the status of a dinner he knew wasn't there, he poked his head into the shabby yellow kitchen. He'd promised to remodel it when he'd been promoted, but there hadn't been time, and he hadn't really felt the inclination. It wasn't like Betty was the same girl to whom he'd made those promises anyway.

The house wasn't that bad. In fact, if Dogleg Bend had an upper crust part of town, this was it, just up the hill from Main Street. It probably began as a foreman's house, a brick single-story, built in the sixties. An aluminum double-car canopy sat on the side, surrounded by grayed lattice. He'd remodeled the living room when they moved in, but most of the place, like the kitchen, still needed to be spruced up.

Nevertheless, Kermit felt lucky to have it. Not so many people had it this good in Dogleg Bend since the last of the underground mines had shut down and the devastation had begun to the south. He felt fortunate to have his job at the West Virginia Department of Highways, so he could afford his mortgage. Before he and Betty got married, he already knew he never wanted to live in a trailer again, like he had with Mom.

He didn't feel lucky this evening, though, and there was a distinct aroma of déjà vu mingling with the nearly full trash. Whatever the odor, it didn't smell like dinner. He wasn't in the mood for Millie's Diner or Totelli's Pizza. There were more choices in Trevelton, but he didn't feel like driving twenty minutes for Chinese or KFC.

He walked back into the living room and stood over Betty. Her mouth hung open and a few strands of her black hair lay across her lips, askew as if she were floating underwater, sucked in and out with the slow tide of her breath. Looking at her, he was reminded of Mom in her housecoat, a bottle of Seagram's on the coffee table. He turned away before the comparisons went any further, before he started considering throwing water in her face and screaming at her.

He walked over, sank into the recliner, switched the channel to ESPN, and cranked the volume.

Nothing.

He unfolded the *Bergen County Gazette* he had carried in with him and looked at the headline for the hundredth time: *GREENBACK CALLS FOUL ON DOH—Claims signs stolen at height of election season.*

Kermit rubbed the bridge of his nose, squinting. What a shitstorm.

Part of him wished that, three days ago, he would have paused to consider the possible repercussions before he sent out the crews to clear illegal signs. If he had done that, he might have reconsidered the whole thing. But his drive to work that day had made the decision for him. The law was being flagrantly violated, and the roads in the county were beginning to look like a dump. Once made, the decision was permanent, petrified into the hardest stone. He would never back down from his choice. He threw the paper across the room, past Betty's head.

Nothing.

He thought she was a real shit for fucking him over on a day like today, and again wished for a normal life, something that didn't seem so much to ask for. He wasn't sure what that might be like. He rose from the chair and stood looking down at her.

He wondered what it was this time, who she got it from. He often wondered this. Old Calvin across the road had told him he'd seen Dewey Burke's car up here a couple times. With its orange door and silver body, it was easy to spot. She probably got her hands on some Oxys, but you can't smell pills. He thought about checking her usual stash places and then decided it wasn't worth it. That would just prompt another fight.

He nudged her shoulder with the back of his hand, nudged again, and then nudged harder. He suppressed the urge to slap her. No matter how bad she got—and every time he asked anything directly, the fight got worse—he could never bring himself to actual physical violence. Her eyes came slowly open and then widened when she saw him. She began to twist, turn, and stretch, her t-shirt riding up over her navel ring.

"Well hey, baby," she said. He remembered when he used to find that drawl sexy, when the look of her roused from sleep was likely to delay her actually getting out of bed.

Not tonight. Tonight, it would be god-awful pizza.

A FEW DAYS before Kermit contemplated pizza, and a day into the sign cleanup, an early morning call from Reverend

Mooney at the Baptist Church had been the first portent that things were about to go horribly awry.

"Well, what I mean, Reverend, and I apologize again for any disrespect, is that while I entirely sympathize with your position, the entire county was given ample notice that these removals were going to take place. My crews were instructed to remove *all* signs in violation of the legal distance and those illegally placed on county or state property. I truly wish that your sign had been moved before my crews set out."

A moment of silence ensued, like church.

"Mr. Hamrick, I really don't think our sign presented a problem."

"Reverend, I'm sorry, but our office has fielded numerous complaints about your sign in particular. It blocked the view when turning from Elizabeth Road."

"This is because of that old Mildred Barnes, isn't it?" Reverend Mooney's voice had risen. "She calls here all the time. Oh, Heaven help us! Mrs. Barnes isn't happy. So, you destroyed our sign on the whims of one cranky *Methodist*?"

"Reverend, this is a county-wide sweep. Like I said, *all* signs in violation of the law are being removed. Not just yours. I will look into whether your sign is salvageable. That's about all I can do for you."

"Mr. Hamrick, this church has been here since 1895. My great-great-grandpappy…"

Kermit's attention strayed. His office manager, Carol Anne, leaned against his doorway, trying to get his attention in a knee-length floral dress, white with purple flowers. She looked like spring, like lust after sunrise service on Easter Sunday. On the phone, the preacher continued his oral history of the church, which wasn't helping Kermit pull his gaze from the curve of Carol Anne's hip. She gestured to the phone. The other line was on hold.

The barrage of phone calls had begun: the Chamber of Commerce, several business owners, and of course, the campaign office of state senator, M. Wallace Greenback.

Kermit walked out of his office that first day and stopped at Carol Anne's desk. "What is it, Carol Anne? Why is it every goddamn person out there thinks they're special and the law doesn't apply to them?"

"'Cause people are assholes, Kermit."

Kermit smiled. He could always count on a straight answer, even if every word did seem loaded now.

"No more calls. I'm done with assholes for the day."

"Okay, Kerm."

Every word.

ON THAT FIRST afternoon, after the initial calls, Kermit wandered out into the yard to wait for the trucks to see if he could at least get the church's sign back. He had no intention of doing that for anyone else. When he saw Walt's truck pulling in, he directed him to dump his load behind the garages. By the time he cleared the corner of the building, the massive pile of signs was already falling from the back of the truck.

He stood there, looking for a minute.

"All of these?" he exclaimed to no one in particular.

The three guys on the crew turned around, grinning.

"I guess it went alright," said Kermit.

"Yeah, Kerm," said Walt, "no problems. The boys here even enjoyed themselves, I think."

"Yeah," said Jimmy Gainor, a gangly twenty-something with a scruffy beard, "it was kind of, well, *relaxing*." Kermit couldn't remember ever seeing him so happy after a day's work. He wondered if the kid was stoned before his attention was pulled back to the four-foot pile of twisted metal, plastic, and broken wood.

"Holy shit. I knew it was a problem, but this? Shit. There must be a hundred signs here, and you're only one crew."

"I feel like I left West Virginia a more beautiful place," said Jimmy, as Kermit, again, wondered.

"You guys did work out by Elizabeth Road, right? Think we can get the Baptist sign outta there? I had a helluva time on the phone with the preacher."

"Aw shit, Kerm," said Walt, "that thing was damn near anchored on the berm. It was deep. We tore the fuck out of it."

"That was when it got kind of fun," said Jimmy.

THAT DAY'S HEADLINE in the *Bergen County Gazette* was not the last. Senator Greenback made a righteous stink in the media over the affront to his free speech during the primary campaign season. Kermit fielded daily calls from his superiors in Charleston. They began as questions and reprimands, but became more supportive when Senator Greenback publicly vowed to change the road sign laws in the next legislative session.

Kermit often thought about the fact that Greenback was unopposed in the primary.

This, in turn, often led him to thinking about the southern third of the county, just over the hill from the DOH yards, all life there ravaged, flattened, gutted by grinning diesel dinosaurs and dynamite, everything else poisoned by the groundwater, barren and riddled with cancer like Betty's family, driven from their home by death.

Kermit recalled Greenback saying that mountaintop removal was a great idea, too. It was going to create jobs, said the Senator on TV, on the radio, in the paper, and on his podium. Apparently, these jobs weren't for anyone Kermit knew. And Kermit knew a lot of people.

AT HOME, TOO, life remained the guessing game that he was entirely sick of playing. Every morning he got up, showered, kissed Betty goodbye, and wondered what condition he would find her in later.

One morning after the cleanup, he left the house with a determined dash through steady rain to where his truck was parked under the canopy next to Betty's Grand Am. At the end of his street, he turned right onto Pike Creek Road, following the path of rain running to the river. He made his way out of the pseudo-suburbs of Dogleg Bend, built atop the very lumber camp that started it all, and onto Route Twelve, which ran through town proper. He turned away from town, left, toward Upper Leg.

The two main parts of town had been referred to for generations as "Upper Leg" and "Lower Leg," corresponding to the river bends along which the town sat. Lower Leg had downtown: the drugstore, the town's two restaurants, the old Ferguson Theater, a couple gas stations, one with a convenience store, and a few other businesses, most closed. All of it was old and dying, paint flaking, stone and brick chipped and dull, or already dead, slowly murdered by the

Walmart on the northeastern outskirts of town, where the dog's paw would have been, though nobody called it that.

Kermit drove south through Upper Leg—less developed, but somehow feeling even more abandoned. The old lumber mill, on the river's edge to his right, had been closed at least fifty years. The roof sagged in the middle. It loomed out of the overgrown fauna and rampant wheat grass like a mammoth sinking into a tar pit. On his left, he passed the old high school, closed when the county schools consolidated to become the new Bergen High up in Trevelton. At least the grounds there were kept up, mostly for the baseball field, but also for the occasional community meetings in the classrooms.

He accelerated as he hit the straight stretch before the hill. The depot road was off to the right, near the top of the long incline. No sooner had he gassed it and the truck leaped forward, he quickly removed his foot from the pedal. He almost passed the thing before it could truly register, but there it was, illegal as hell, mounted on two metal sign posts, a long, green, rectangular sign. ROTWEILER PUPS— FREE! He was too incensed to register the phone number beneath.

He accelerated again along the straightaway and out past the last of the sparsely peppered structures, all run down like old dogs. He pondered who the culprit or culprits might be as he drove the last few tree-lined miles before turning onto the access road to the depot. Whoever it was obviously didn't read the paper.

Kermit often observed that the State Road depot yard, in the greater dog-leg picture, sat just below where the dog's ass would be, but nobody called it that.

CAROL ANNE ALREADY had the coffee brewing when he came in wet. It wouldn't do any good to ask her if she'd seen the sign, because she always drove in on Corwin Road.

"Carol Anne, if you see Walt before me, tell him I got a job for him."

"I'll do it," she sang.

"You're awfully chipper this morning."

"Well, only 'cause I been thinking about puppies." She offered a smile both innocent and mischievous and set a cup of coffee on his desk in front of the picture of him and Betty at the beach. She always set it there now.

"Puppies?"

"Ain't it funny?" she asked. "We had two different people call here this morning asking about free puppies. I told them if they figured out where the free Rottweilers were, to give *me* a call. Those dogs are like eight hundred dollars, you know."

"What do you need a Rottweiler for?" he asked, barely thinking about the words coming out of his mouth. His mind was putting the sign, the phone number, and Carol Anne all together and, even in the light of his dawning realization, he still found himself sidetracked by the thought of his lips on the side of her neck.

"Well, maybe if I had a big, strong man to take care of me." She trailed off, her eyebrows arching. Carol Anne was divorced and lived by herself in a trailer just off Corwin. He'd only been inside it one time, after the Christmas party, when she needed a ride. She kept it nice, for a trailer.

The phone rang and Carol Anne turned around, giving him another long look as she walked back to her desk.

"Puppies?" he heard her say. "Isn't that strange? You're the third person to call about puppies this morning."

Kermit frowned.

TONIGHT, IT WAS hot dogs, pork and beans, and macaroni and cheese, the straight noodle variety.

"Sorry, babe," she said. "It's all we had in the house."

He gave her a reassuring smile. The real talking had ended a few years back, but he understood, in retrospect, that their talk had never been about much of anything, just two kids imagining their version of the good life.

He looked at his cheap wiener wrapped in a slice of Wonder Bread and considered the good life before he bit into it.

She was such a sexy thing back then, just ten short years ago. Oh, she hadn't lost her figure, those short, shapely legs, the perfect breasts for her small frame. It wasn't a physical thing at all. The light had just gone out of those brown eyes. She still smiled, pranced, and danced about, but Kermit had learned that it was all a big show. She was trying to convince herself as much as she was trying to convince everyone around her.

He smiled and pretended too. There was no way forward that he could see. He ate his powdered cheese macaroni and feigned satisfaction. There was an edge to her joy tonight.

IN THE WEEKS following the free puppy sign, numerous people called the depot asking about the free tractor that needed work, or how much free topsoil was available, even one for suicide prevention. Carol Anne was rattled by that one. She talked to the unemployed coal miner's wife while she looked up a real suicide prevention hotline. Afterward, she was shaking. Kermit hugged her until the pressure of her fingers on his back forced him to cut it short.

He dispatched a couple trucks to canvas the county roads, find the outlaw signs, and bring them to the justice of the junkyard. Again, he wondered who was behind all this. He wanted to blame the preacher or one of his congregants.

"TWO hundred dollars!" the pastor had said over and over, like it was some spell or chant that could make the money magically reappear in his hands, if only he didn't stop saying it. Kermit apologized for not being able to retrieve the church's sign, but didn't feel sorry about disappointing the reverend. The church had since put up a new one, bigger and better, and probably within a frog hair of the line. The complaints from Mildred Barnes were sure to begin again. Yes, he could quite easily see the preacher dropping a broad hint to a member of his congregation.

Short of sending out the sign brigade, he didn't have time for much else in way of investigating. He had raw material inventory that day and a meeting with his two schedulers about spring fills. That was also the day that Greenback chose to declare the Department of Highways to be a den of nepotism and Democratic Party conspirators. That afternoon, the news trucks began showing up at the depot.

Kermit did three television interviews that day, first with a station from Charleston, then Clarksburg, then Wheeling. He was asked questions like, "Did you receive instructions to tear down the political signs of Senator Greenback?" Kermit explained calmly that this was a fair, county-wide sweep, initiated by the county office, and that the Senator's signs were not the only ones removed. He reiterated the state law and returned often to the statement, "I'm sure we can all agree that safety is important on West Virginia highways."

He tacked on a joke at the end about West Virginia highways being more scenic now, but Kermit still thought they all left a little disappointed.

Two of the DOH trucks came back near quitting time empty-handed. The last truck to arrive was Walt's. Jimmy Gainor jumped out and yelled, "We found the free tractor sign!"

The next morning, they got a call for an abortion clinic.

KERMIT'S SUPERVISOR IN Charleston called him the next morning as well.

"Hamrick," he said, "saw you on the news last night. You should've called us, let us know."

"Yeah, sorry about that, Ted, but they surprised me. It just happened. I didn't really have time to think. I hope I didn't screw anything up."

"No, no, nothing like that. You did fine. That bastard Greenback is setting himself up for a run at the Governor's seat and he's just trying to get some free publicity at our expense. Said it was a plot of the entrenched Democratic regime in state government. He's grandstanding—but listen—that's only partly why I called."

"Oh?"

"Well, you looked good on TV, Hamrick. Made the DOH look real good. Senator Nelson is planning to convene a special session of the legislature here in a few weeks, trying to regain control of the conversation or some shit like that.

He wants you to come down to Charleston to testify. You up to it? We'll arrange for some comp time for you, pay to put you up."

"I guess so."

"Good," said Dempsey, "and don't be surprised if you get a call from one of my friends, George Pelton. He wants to talk to you."

The next call was indeed from George Pelton, a member of the Democratic Party, asking him if he ever thought about running for House of Delegates. The call after that was from old Calvin, who lived across the street from him.

HE SPED DOWN Route Twelve, toward home, the rundown barns and shacks and mills falling apart as he flew by, fractured and dissolved by the water in his eyes.

Losing the third one. That's when it happened.

Or maybe, it all started before that even, when Betty lost her father and sister. She always swore it was all on account of what happened to her family's water when they started blasting Spenser Mountain. But it wasn't until after the third miscarriage that she'd started complaining about the pain. Soon after that came the OxyContin. When that became a problem, the parade of anti-depressants began, one after another. None of them ever robbed her of her taste for the OxyContin. She liked the oblivion they brought. It was as though she wanted to knock herself right out of the world the way those babies were knocked out of her womb.

He supposed he bore some of the blame. After the second miscarriage, he'd had a hard time getting back to a supportive place. Betty was constantly on about the coal company and her sister's cancer, and Kermit, tiring of it, started blaming her a little. When he saw her after the third, sobbing in her hospital bed, he knew that they were doomed, but he couldn't bring himself to leave her like that.

He realized he was crying now, because it was Mom all over again, in so many ways. Was it true that you just had to keep repeating things over and over in your life? Was there no escape? From the time he'd been old enough to understand, he tried to help her, begged her, pleaded with her, got angry with her, but the bottle always called her back. She never did come to terms with Dad's death and Kermit never could get her to come back. In the end, he watched her die, eaten by cirrhosis at forty-five, a shell of a woman who never came to grips with being alone. He watched her die now, again, in his mind, and his fury grew.

And then, there it was, right as he turned onto Pike Creek Road, a sign with the DOH depot phone number that read, "FORTUNES TOLD." Kermit couldn't take it. He whipped his truck off the road and jumped out, going at the metal fence posts with his Redwings like a shitkicker Kung-Fu madman, screaming that all assholes should stop being assholes.

The sign wasn't going anywhere though, and several cars had passed by. He composed himself for the walk back to his truck.

WHEN HE EXPLODED into the house, Betty's reactions were slow, off by a second. It took a moment for the accusation to sink in.

"No!" she screamed. "I never done that. I never done that!" She ran her fingers backward over her skull, through her hair.

"Calvin saw you coming out of her house. And she's obviously not home!" Kermit's arms pointed to Mrs. Sanders house next door.

"Oh, that old geezer is seeing things."

He wanted to hit her. Every part of him wanted to slap her.

"That old geezer sees better'n you do." Kermit sneered at her. "Fucked up all the time."

"Are you saying you don't believe me?" Tears welled in her eyes now, part of the show.

"What was in there? Huh? Some valium, maybe? I doubt Mrs. Sanders has Oxys, but you *are* looking pretty lit up, so you found something. What'd you find, Betty?"

"Oh, what the fuck difference does it make anyway? You don't believe me. You never did. I might as well be dead, too."

She started throwing things, pillows first, then lamps and remotes and anything else she could get her hands on. It ended like it always did, with Betty sobbing and Kermit holding her. He really did love her once.

But later that evening, he lay in bed, thinking about a winter night, warm, wine-soaked breath on his neck, soft flesh and loving eyes reflecting the warm luminescence of Christmas lights, and the fact that alcohol can make a trailer floor into the most romantic spot in the world.

IN THE MORNING, he donned his usual attire: dress shirt, pair of jeans, his Redwings. Betty was up. She had breakfast for him today. He declined, pleading lateness. He was lying.

Betty offered a pity-me look, meant to be sexy.

"You be good today," Kermit said.

"I will," she said.

She was lying too, he knew.

He drove to work, lighter. Something had clicked inside of him, a kind of resolve that he hadn't felt before. Something big was imminent. Change seemed inevitable. As he hit the straightaway on Route 12, he saw it up ahead, another sign too close to the road. Coming up on it, he could see it was more than one sign. In fact, it was three in all, stacked to be read like the shaving cream signs on Route 66.

YOU CAN'T KEEP

A GOOD SIGN

DOWN

No, he thought, maybe you can't. At least the assholes had a sense of humor.

He didn't know it yet, but Carol Anne had already taken two of many more calls to come inquiring about the free full body massage. She would make a suggestive joke about that later and he would ask her to travel to Charleston with him. It would be a long time before he found out who was responsible for the signs.

The hill before the depot rose in front of him. The crest—where the trees had been cleared away and the road met the blue sky—cut a sharp line, like a doorway to the edge of the world, like maybe if you hit that edge, you might just keep on going right on into the sky, right on into the next life.

Report on the Strange Case of Lt. Henry Harper

Professor Bixby,

I am emailing you from my room in the Motel 6 outside of Trevelton, WV. I am tired and still jumpy from the events of the last couple days. So far, I feel as if my trip has been less than the treasure hunt I was expecting, but I still have hope that there will be enough useful research for an interesting thesis. The digital recorder you loaned me turned out to be invaluable in gathering what little relevant material I was able to accrue. I wish I could tell you that we could use more of what I recorded in Dogleg Bend, West Virginia.

As you know, I had no way of contacting Mr. Harper before I left for Dogleg Bend. I had sketchy information on his military service and Japanese imprisonment from my talks with Mrs. Valerie Coleman, his estranged daughter who lives in Morgantown. It's a fascinating story, to be sure, and I was most anxious to talk to the lieutenant himself.

Mrs. Coleman informed me that her father lived as a hermit out in the middle of nowhere and that she couldn't attest to his current mental state. She seemed to be implying he was crazy and there was a tone in her voice I didn't care for, maybe because I lost my own father so early. I never really knew my own father, but I've told you about that.

I knew about Harper's reclusive nature. I knew also that, after the war, he emerged briefly as an artist with promising reviews, but according to Mrs. Coleman, her father "did not want to play that game." I knew that he turned ninety-six this year. I knew all of this and still, surprises remained.

The first of these greeted me the day I arrived in Dogleg Bend. The area is scenic enough in the spring, especially with the dogwood and cherry blossoms, but I suspect every pollinating plant lurking in those hills had it out for me. My allergies were insufferable. The GPS unit led me to what I believed to be the correct route, Slipback Road, but shortly out that way, I came upon two young men, somewhere near my age, I think, who were erecting a "live bait" sign next to the road. When I asked them if they knew how to find Mr. Harper's place, the one with the toothpick in his mouth informed me that an upcoming bridge had washed out, giving me directions so convoluted that I ended up lost for three hours. There was no bridge washed out, I discovered.

I finally found Henry Harper's property around 1:30 that afternoon. I turned up the dirt road next to the mailbox, and soon, sculptures materialized on the side of the road: an old boiler, painted solid black with rust spots and pipes emerging from its sides like titan arms. A clawed bathtub with a shower spigot rising from one end like the leg of a lawn flamingo, propped against a tree as if resting there, drooping its spigot-head, asleep. All the way up the winding driveway, it was like being on the grounds of a junk museum, an impression undiminished as the main dwelling came into view.

A slanted acre of open field spread out behind the cabin which had been there a long time, not dilapidated, just old, the wood gray and splintering, patched in spots with what looked to be tar. Other than a few junk piles in the dirt yard, the place looked cozy. Higher on the hillside, to the left of the dwelling and set perpendicular, perched a gray double-wide trailer, not as sturdy-looking as the cabin. It sat on a narrow, flat spot that looked like it had been bulldozed into the side of the hill. It drooped slightly in the middle. Behind the cabin, in front of the field which stretched out from there, stood several wind sculptures, a metal shed and a medium-sized barn, perhaps a workshop, or a garage, or both. On the left side of the property loomed an outhouse that I hoped was for decoration (it wasn't). And everywhere, on all sides, the tangled woods. The large trees here and there on the property made it feel like the woods were leaning in, about to devour everything.

Henry Harper sat on the front porch on a wooden rocker next to a cable spool he was using for a table. He was unfazed by my arrival, not that you could tell what was going on under that great beard from any distance. He spoke as I stepped out of the car, his voice a cracked, raggedy bell.

"Well, you ain't a coal man. I can tell that by the looks of ya."

"Henry Harper?" I asked.

"That'd be me. You ain't a gas man, neither."

I was self-conscious under his scrutiny. There was a sharpness in those blue eyes, peeking out from all that gray-white facial fur. All that hair made his head look too big for his body. I've attached pictures to this email, and I think you'll agree that he looks like the quintessential mountain man, an image belied by the frailty and slightness of his frame.

"No sir," I answered.

"Well, if ya didn't drive such a crappy vehicle, I might think you was a lawyer sent by my kin to declare me *non compos mentis.*" He started laughing.

Harper's voice had me utterly entranced, the thick West Virginia accent and the high, soft tones like gentle gravel. When the words "*non compos mentis*" came out of that little old man, well, it just sparked cognitive dissonance in my mind. It was like opening the Sunday paper to see Snuffy Smith speaking Hebrew.

"No," I said, "I'm a grad student at Clairton College, doing research."

"Researcher. Huh." His posture stiffened, his mouth drew tight. "Then you best set off down the road there, sonny. Joe told me to just send you fellers packin."

"What?" I wondered if someone else was planning a similar paper.

"Joe says all the measuring and defining don't amount to nothin, and that y'all ought to be payin attention to your own selves. Now take yer cameras and yer motion sensors and yer parabolic microphones and git!"

Parabolic microphones? My confusion increased and I was having trouble forming a coherent response. I reached into my jacket pocket and held out the digital recorder.

"All I brought was this," I said, blinking, desperate.

"Do what?" he asked, his fuzzy brow furrowing. He was beginning to look as confused as me.

"Oh, I brought a digital camera, but you don't have to have your picture taken."

"Just why would ya want *my* picture?"

"Because you're a war hero?"

He squinted. "I ain't no hero. And you aren't here to talk about Joe, are ya?"

"I don't know who Joe is. I'm here to ask you about your service in World War Two."

"Well," he said, shoulders relaxing, "now there's something I ain't talked about in a while." A hint of weary inevitability weaved in and out of his words.

When I sat down on the porch, I pulled out a map of Kyushu and asked him if he could show me where he was imprisoned.

He pointed at his chest.

Then at his head.

Already, I knew something was deeply askew.

Even now, listening to that old guy's voice on tape makes me feel like I'm hanging from a breaking limb above a vast canyon, or falling into the void of the industrial bedspread with its thick pattern of orange and white blossoms and green leaves. The darn thing keeps drawing my eye, like it moves of its own accord. Maybe you can begin to see how this visit affected me. As for whether I have obtained useful material for my paper, I'll let you read the transcription and decide for yourself.

(Begin Segment 1)8

DESMOND MOSS: MARCH 30, 2008. This is Desmond Moss, interviewing Lieutenant Henry Harper…[pause]…sir, could you tell me where you served in World War Two?

Henry Harper: I was in the 26th Photo Reconnaissance Squadron in the Pacific, and we was in several places, Australia first. Saw me my first kangaroo there. Then, we moved on to New Guinea and spent a while there, too.

DM: And what were your duties?

HH: Well sir, I'd lay on my belly in the nose of a B-25 with a Kodak camera and snap lovely little pictures of islands and boats and soldiers and airstrips and such.

DM: How often did you fly these missions? Do you remember any specific targets?

HH: Well, me and Walter was about the best photographers, so we went up the most, probably once every two or three days. There was always something to take pictures of. I don't really remember the itty-bitty details no more except for the last one.

DM: July 31, 1944?

HH: Aya, that sounds about right.

DM: Your plane was shot down that day.

HH: Aya, that day, we were lookin' for a couple Japanese destroyers that nobody could account fer. We didn't have no escort 'cause there weren't no reason to think we'd find trouble that far out. But one of the carriers must have been close, and we ran into a squadron of Zeros. And one B-25 up against ten Zeros stands no chance 'tall.

DM: You were the only survivor. Can you tell me about that experience?

HH: No…no, I spec not. That ain't a day I dwell on. Them boys was my friends. I'd like to move on if I had my druthers.

DM: Sure. The records indicate that you were fished out of the East China Sea by the Japanese cruiser, *Sendai Maru*?

HH: I spec. I never knew the name of the boat. It weren't a pleasant experience on that bucket. Them was five of the scariest days of my life right there. I figured 'em to pitch me overboard to the sharks for sure. I ain't never felt that kinda hate put on me, before or since.

DM: But they took you to Japan.

HH: Aya, but I could'na told you then whether I was there, or in China, or what, least not right away.

DM: You were held in Fukuoka #17, from which your daughter says you escaped.

HH: My daughter! I'm surprised she'd talk about me at all [laughs].

DM: Is there any truth to that story, then?

HH: As far as any story, I reckon [laughs].

(*I pause the transcription here for a moment because it occurs to me that I have not described this laugh. If I have time tonight, I'll see if I can edit one out and send you an mp3. It's a cattle-drive cook's laugh, a crazy high cackle that would sound just right after someone says, "These are some mighty fine beans, Cookie."*)

DM: But that's incredible. I can't believe there wasn't a big deal made of it. I mean, nobody escaped from the Japanese prison camps.

HH: Oh, nobody wanted to make a big deal outta me, that's for sure. I didn't fit the mold. Hell, the whole town here thought I was a traitor. I suspect my superiors did as well.

DM: Your daughter said you are a Buddhist, that you came home a Buddhist. Is this why they thought you were a traitor?

HH: My daughter. She's just like her mother, heh, but aya.

DM: She said her mother divorced you because you were a crazy, godless heathen with no normal Christian values.

HH: Shows you how much she knows. But I guess what she said is true enough. I'm a semi-authentic West Virginny

Buddhist hillbilly, alright [laughs]…least I pretend to be, to myself. Joe says from what he knows, I do a passable job of it, pretendin', that is.

DM: Joe, you mentioned him. Who's Joe?

HH: Well looky there…[laughs]

(End Segment 1)

MR. HARPER WAS sidetracked by a vehicle approaching quickly up the dirt road, a silver Civic, an older model, with an orange door on the passenger side. It slid to a stop, and who got out but those two knuckleheads that sent me out to the middle of nowhere.

"Who's yer *friend*, Henry?"

Mr. Harper explained who I was, while the one with the toothpick just stood there, staring at me, burning holes in me with his eyes. I wondered if it was the same toothpick as he'd had earlier. When Henry finished, the two looked at each other and grinned as Henry said to me, "This here's Ned and Dewey. They do odd jobs for me."

"Well," said bait farmer number one, "I guess he weren't a gas man after all, Dewey."

"No," said Mr. Toothpick, "I guess not."

Ned said, "We'll be out in the barn, Henry. Gonna play with the airbrush some more. If you *need* us," he said this like they were leaving Mr. Harper in the hands of a Bible salesman, "you just holler." Dewey just kept *staring* at me, leering, as they walked around toward the barn. I wanted to get to my hotel. I looked at my watch; it was nearly five o'clock.

"You had enough, young fella?"

"It's been a long day. May I come back tomorrow?

"Aya, and if ya like, there's a nice enough bed up in the trailer that yer welcome to use tonight."

From the barn, one of the hooligans exclaimed, "Free hookers!" and then they laughed.

"No, thanks." I said. "All my things are at the hotel. I need to go back."

"Just so ya know. The offer's open."

I SAT DOWN with Lt. Harper the following morning, on his back porch this time. It too had two wooden chairs and a cable spool. I will admit, it was a pleasant place to look out on the morning.

(Begin Segment 2)

DM: WE WERE talking about your escape. Your daughter said something about a Buddhist monk helping you make it to China.

HH: I don't deny it.

DM: Most of the Buddhist sects in Japan at that time supported the war, supported the emperor. How did you get *a monk* to help you?

HH: I didn't get nobody to do nothin'…that's the part most people never understood.

[subject pauses and leans over the table, looking at me with an intensity that made me quite uncomfortable.]

HH: But some things are bigger than world wars, eh? Bigger'n emperors and armies, right [smiles]? That's not what they teach ya up in the college, I know, but that don't make it less true. Ricky knew it.

DM: Ricky?

HH: Aya, Riku. That was his name. And ain't that just a mouthful there? Not so much that there's a bunch of it as it's just odd on the tongue, ya know? [laughs, pauses]…he got a kick outta me callin' him Ricky. And, as for your question: Ricky, he didn't care so much about the war. Wars come and go, same as emperors and governments. No, Ricky, he was more interested in the bigger picture. I guess that's why he became a monk in the first place, wouldn't ya say? [laughs]

DM: He spoke English?

HH: Aya, he'd spent some years in San Francisco.

DM: So not a young man?

HH: [laughs] No, sir, hardly young. Ricky was already an old man when he found me. He served a small temple near the camp, only seven monks there when I saw it. Ricky said there had been fifteen, but that eight had gone into the military. Only the older monks remained.

DM: You say he found you? How did that happen? Was he looking for you?

HH: [laughs] No. [laughs again] No, I was a surprise, ya might say. [laughs again] Ricky had no idea he was lookin' for me till he saw me marching to that camp. And acourse, I didn't know he was lookin' for me neither, not for another eight months.

DM: I'm not sure I understand.

HH: Well, it's like I said, some things are bigger than wars, son. Some things are deep and mysterious, and we wonder how they could happen at all. When Ricky saw me, when he looked into my eyes, he knew he'd been lookin' for me. That's all. It's just that simple.

DM: And yet, he didn't help you escape for another eight months? Did it take him that long to formulate a plan?

HH: [laughs] You got it wrong there. Just 'cause Ricky knew he'd been looking for me didn't mean he started plotting my escape. [laughs] No, Ricky was a man of intelligence, and he did what any smart man would do: he let it go. But as fortune would have it, and luckily for me, it didn't let go of *him*. It was another eight months in that hellhole, though, before I even knew who Ricky was.

DM: Can you tell me about Fukuoka #17?

HH: What's to tell? You know, my Papaw owned the lumbermill down by the river. It was always expected that I would have an easier life than those around me. And what happens? [laughs] I end up in a coal mine in Japan! [laughs] Halfway around the world from West Virginia…and I end up in a coal mine…[pause]…you ain't saying nothin'…[pause]…well, I don't know I got anything you couldn't get nowheres else, but twelve-hour days in that hole…thirty minutes to eat whatever rations that chickenshit k-p officer saw fit to give ya, and he was corrupt as the day is long. I heard they court-martialed him later—an American, heh! Some things teach ya that nothing's clear.

What else ya want? Diarrhea? Malaria? Pneumonia? I was one of the lucky ones. Even luckier that I got out…[pauses again, longer; looks out to the open field behind his cabin]…I don't know what tellin' ya all this really helps with in the long run. You know, Ol' Stinky Joe, he says we got the flaws of our makers, that it's not entirely our fault, we was set up to lose. There'll always be another war, another Fukuoka, no matter what.

DM: Old Stinky Joe. Oh, the Joe you spoke of earlier? Who is that?

HH: Joe's an old friend. Sometimes, he comes down from the high places and we have tea.

DM: Did you know him from the war?

HH: No. Maybe. [laughs] I don't know. All I know is I'm a might peckish. What say we have some lunch?

(End Segment 2)

WE ATE DINTY Moore beef stew on a kitchen table with tapered metal legs, capped with metal disks. The tabletop had faded Formica flowers, direct from the 1970s. It wobbled.

But the inside of the cabin wasn't dirty. It was open, with hardwood floor and a fireplace in the middle. The kitchen had running water and an old refrigerator. There were books, lots of them, on shelves near the corner where his bed sat, but it felt too much like snooping in someone's bedroom to take a closer look at those.

We continued our conversation later that afternoon, but were immediately interrupted by the two ne'er-do-wells. They waved as they loped by, Dewey smirking at me the entire time, and headed straight to the barn. I wondered what they were really doing in there.

(Begin Segment 3)

DM: I'D LIKE to go back to your escape. It's such a fascinating story.

HH: Aya, I guess that's one waya lookin' at it…or maybe just one of those things, ya know? Ricky told me it was just one of those weird moments when he first laid eyes on me, but he didn't judge its worth. He waited for the world to tell him what it meant. Then, a couple months later, he started dreaming about it, and, even then, he had no reason to be anywhere near me.

But this here's how the world works sometimes. One of the work detail guards, a feller by the name of Yukio, was a former monk from Riku's temple, and he was having some troubles adapting to his new job. Probably something about prisoners being slowly starved and worked to death, if I had to guess. But eventually, he sent word to the temple that he wished some counsel from his old master, Riku. Ricky arrived at the mine when the prisoner shift was changing, as it happened. While he waited on Yukio lining up the next detail, here I come, up out of the earth, looking like the raised dead. I don't know how he even recognized me under all that coal dust, but he did, and that was it for Ricky. That was when he knew for sure he was looking for me.

He visited Yukio at the mine regularly for nearly a month before we got the chance to speak. I was waiting in line for the last shift to get topside so we could board the lift when Ricky came up behind me.

American? he asked.

Now, it kinda threw me, him speaking English, but I didn't say nothin'. I was afraida being punished for talking to him, so I just nodded. I kept looking down, and then all around, afraid someone would see me. Then, he asked me a peculiar question.

What is sound of one hand clapping? [pauses and rubs his forehead]

Now, I can't say quite how that question hit me. Like a rock hittin' the bottom of a deep well, maybe. It threw me, son, I tell ya. I wanted to laugh, but I was terrified. And, just wanting him to get away from me, I whispered, kinda nasty-like, [whispers] *A lot like the sound of being thrown in the box!* [laughs] Well, ol' Ricky, it took him a second or two to comprehend my meaning, but when he did, his mouth rounded into an O, his eyebrows raised and his eyes just dancing. He pointed at me and began walking away, just laughing to beat the band.

Not long after, maybe a week, Yukio snuck me around behind the tool shed at the mine, where Ricky was waiting with monk robes, and that was it.

DM: But why? It seems incredible to me. Such a risk. Why did he do it?

HH: Well, son, it's like I said, some things are bigger than danger. Some loyalties run deeper than the illusion of death. Some folk out there believe that we're surrounded by the spirits that are important to us, whether we see em or not. Riku…well, Riku, he just happened to look up one day and see one, right there in front of him.

DM: A spirit?

HH: Aya, [laughs] riding around in the body of a skinny hillbilly, marching to the coal mines.

DM: I'm not sure I understand

HH: [laughs] Does anybody, really, do ya think? [laughs] I know *I* didn't and I'm not sure Ricky did either. He told me that when he looked into my eyes, he saw the eyes of his old teacher, Hiroyuki, who had died many years before. The old coot sure seemed surprised, confused, and delighted about the whole thing. When I told him there weren't nobody insida me but me, he bowed, for cryin' out loud! [laughs] Told me I was still very wise, grinnin' like a fool.

DM: It's just so hard to believe, all that stuff.

HH: That's just the kinda feller you are, idn't it? Everything has its place and time. Everything is set in stone. No room for change. For lookin' at things different.

DM: I'm not a revisionist, no.

HH: Aya, didn't think so. Son, there ain't nothin' in your life that made you question the way you thought things was? Nothin 'tall?

DM: No sir. [HH scrutinizes me like he's looking at the air around me]

HH: Uh-huh. You know, sometimes, you have to give yourself permission to dream, son. Sometimes, you have to let go of the things you've learned so you can see things as they are.

DM: So then, you believe that you are this Hiro—

HH: Hiroyuki? Aaa…[waves hand]…I don't know one way or another, and what's it matter? All I knew was that Riku was my friend, my good friend. It don't happen often I think, but sometimes, recognition is a two-way street. I knew I could trust him deep down and it made me want to listen to him, learn from him. I spent a month hiding in that temple, so there weren't much left to do but talk to Ricky about being and nothingness and learn about mindfulness and how to meditate.

DM: How did you get out of there?

HH: One night, Ricky wakes me, says it's time for an exercise in mindfulness, and loads me into the back of a truck with two cows! [laughs] Spend a few hours in the back of a moving truck with two cows sometime and see if it ain't the truth. [laughs] They drove me south, to a temple in Nagasaki, a beautiful place that I only ever saw in moonlight. Isn't that somethin? I'll always remember it in moonlight. Ricky stayed with me, but I still had to keep out of sight, even more so. I spent another month hiding there, while Ricky arranged things. Sometimes, Ricky's friend, Masato, would come and sit with me and just smile at me—he didn't speak no English. Then, Ricky would return and the two of 'em would just jibber and jabber and laugh and grin at me. They were the grinninest folks I ever seen. I tell ya, it was strange, no doubt, for a young man who only had a picture of crazy, kamikaze-type Japanese before this. See? Sometimes, you have to forget what you've learned.

DM: How did you get off the islands and to China?

HH: A three-sailed junk, my boy. Prettiest ship I ever laid eyes on. All greens and gold and dark brown. I stayed in a compartment below until we were out to sea, and then, I was finally allowed out to see daylight again.

DM: And you made it across unchallenged?

HH: Well, by this time, the Japanese were pulling a lot of their troops off the mainland. The war was going badly for them all the way around. Riku moved the cows to the temple in Nagasaki because people were going hungry and the cows were safer there. By the time we boarded the junk, Japanese surrender was a foregone conclusion. A couple times, we were stopped on the water, but really, they had better things to do than harass monks.

(End Segment 3)

AFTER EATING SOME pizza that I bought, we sat out on Henry's porch again and watched the evening fade from the night sky. This was the latest I'd yet stayed, and it seemed like Mr. Harper was enjoying my company. He invited me to spend the night again and pointed up to the double-wide that sat above the cabin.

"It don't look like much," he said, "but it's clean, there's electricity, and a nice bed. Just don't try to use the bathroom in there. That don't work too good."

Honestly, I should have said no, but we were getting on so well, and I was so excited about the prospect of his tale and what it might mean to my research, that I accepted.

"The boys call that the 'Love Shack,'" he said, laughing. Already, I was regretting my choice.

But that seemed to engage the gears again, and out there in the mountain dark, with the Milky Way stretched out before us, I managed to steer him back on subject.

(Begin Segment 4)

DM: YOU SAID you sailed to mainland China on a junk?

HH: Aya, took us four days to get over there on that boat, which was fine with me. On the boat, I could be in the open more, and I was enjoying the taste of freedom. Riku had already warned me that the journey through China would be difficult, and I got ready to live under the stars again.

DM: Where did you land?

HH: North of Shanghai, where Riku's acquaintance, a fellow monk, took charge of me and we began our overland journey south to Kunming…[pauses]…that was the last time I ever spoke with brother Ricky.

DM: You never tried to contact him after the war?

HH: Well, now, that'd been kinda difficult…[pauses]…you see, Riku went back to Nagasaki, where he planned to spend some more time at the temple and visit his family.

DM: So, he was there when—

HH: Aya, he was…[pauses]…because of me, and after all he did for me. [wipes tears from his eyes] Ya know, we took a page from the Chinese on that one, right out of Sun Tzu. We did the unthinkable, for no other reason than to let the rest of the world know we could. Never forgave Truman for that one. Never will.

[It was obvious the subject needed a few minutes. I obliged him.]

HH: I think I'm done with the good old days for tonight. You know, now I remember again why I hate talking about that time. For a little while there, I thought it might be important, telling you this story…

DM: It *is* important, for the future.

HH: Nah, it ain't. What are you taking down there on that little machine? What's it going to be? Some numbers in a study, I'll warrant. What's truest from my life will never make it through into your study. Dates, numbers, certainty. This happened, then that. Some things ain't important at all. That moth fluttering by the window over there is every bit as important as any thing I ever done or saw.

DM: I don't understand.

HH: And there you go. That's our curse, you know. Joe's always said it and I never saw nothing would set me to thinkin' different. Our gift from the gods, insane pride. Ain't nothing as good as us.

DM: Again, Joe…I'd like to know more about Joe. He sounds interesting.

HH: [gives me a look—skeptical] Aya. That's one way of putting it.

DM: Did I hear you call him stinky?

HH: He's a tad musky, aya. Likely you won't ever see him, though I'd wager it'd be good for ya.

DM: Why not?

HH: He don't care much for categorizers, for namers. Joe don't have no category.

DM: But he has a name.

HH: Just the one I gave him and the ones given to him by others. Ain't nothin' in a name… [pauses]…there's some people up north claim to share my name. You met one of 'em. They think that name entitles 'em to somethin'. They'd like nothing better than to get their hands on my land so they could sell the rest of this mountain to the coal company and become important rich folks…[subject pauses, then smiles at me in the dark]…but want don't mean nothin', neither. Some things are bigger than names, than families, and wars, and coal companies, right? Some things are bigger than nuclear bombs.

(End Segment 4)

Henry Harper fell quiet after that, pensive, and I didn't want to disturb him. I told him good night, excused myself, and, carrying the flashlight he gave me, made my way up to the "Love Shack."

THE FIRST THING I saw when I entered the trailer was the bed. It sat in the room meant to be the living area, under a bay window that looked out at the side of a hill, no more than fifteen feet away. A heater made to look like a fireplace sat under the mantle in front of plastic stone wall covering. On the mantel, on the headboard, on the bay window shelf, and on the nightstand, were colorful rivers of hardened wax, the remnants of old candles, dripping forever off the sides, pooled in perpetuity. To my surprise, the bed linens were clean. I was relieved, but still reluctant to climb in, just imagining what earned the trailer its name.

That was when I was struck by two other things. One, the painting which hung on the wall opposite the bed, and two, the hundreds of rolled canvases and stacks of drawings filling up every corner of the room.

The painting on the wall was in oil. An amazingly realistic depiction of the view from Henry Harper's back porch. It was as though it had been painted in the light of just this morning. Every grass stalk, every wildflower, everything that swayed and lived between Henry Harper's back porch and the edge of the woods, was captured with complete perfection. The picture became murkier at the wood line, subtle entanglements just out of sight, and just in front of the branches, in a corner of that field, a figure drew my gaze. Someone stood in shadow.

Rolled canvases stuck out of umbrella stands, buckets, old trash cans, and cardboard tubes and boxes. I couldn't resist unrolling them, one after another. In two hours, I barely scratched the surface. Exhausted, I bit my lip and fell into bed. I'm a little embarrassed to admit I left the light on. There are a lot of noises in the mountains at night. I looked at the picture on the wall, trying to decipher the meaning of the figure by the woods, until I finally fell asleep.

Not an hour later, I woke to the sound of scuttling noises just outside the trailer. My eyes flew open like spring-roller blinds, all the way up, spinning and flapping. I listened, unable to move, not knowing where to move, as the handle on the door began to turn. I'm ashamed to say, I might have squealed just a little as those two troublemakers burst into the room, running straight at me and leaping for the bed.

They landed on either side of me, pinning me beneath the covers, and I could immediately smell the alcohol on their breath. I turned first toward Dewey, now smirking drunkenly.

"So, professor," he said, leaning in toward me, "you ever kiss a *man* before?"

The new implications of the name, "Love Shack," knocked the world out from under me. Suddenly, I was falling, my stomach left behind. I turned to the other one, Ned, hoping, I guess, that he would save me from his friend. He held up a twelve-pack of Milwaukee's Best and raised his eyebrows.

"We brought beer!" he exclaimed .

I tried to break free of the blankets, but Dewey held me down with his forearm.

"'Cause you know, Ned and me, we both kissed a man before, so we want to know and you got to tell us. Have you *ever* kissed a *man* before?"

"No." It was a croak, for crying out loud.

"Well then, it's high time you had a beer, professor," said Ned, cracking open a can and shoving it in my face. "Drink up!"

I didn't know what else to do but stall for time. I took the beer and drank it while they sat there and, in very animated fashion, related the intimate details of their sexual conquests in that very bed. Amongst other things, I learned that Peg Bisset has a heart-shaped birthmark, perfect enough to be a tattoo, right above her "boosh."

"I think that *is* a tattoo, Dewey."

"Nah, she told me it weren't."

"I think she was pulling yer leg, amongst other things."

"Speaking of pulling things," Dewey said, looking at me trapped between them and the headboard. "Give the professor another beer, Ned."

"Sure thing, brother."

Dewey fiddled with his belt buckle.

"I'm—not—a professor—yet" I said. My breath was coming in short hitches. I felt my beer can hand trembling.

"What?" they said it together.

"I'm just—a grad student." They looked at each other and started laughing

"Tonight," said Ned, handing me another can, "You are the Professor of Drinking Beer."

"And the Professor of Looooooooove," said Dewey.

I plotted my escape. I'd crash through the bay window behind me, cuts and gashes be damned, and run down over the hill to the car.

It wasn't going to happen.

I tilted the second can and took a big drink in the bizarre hope they might start to like me and forget all about raping me in a double-wide in the middle of nowhere.

"Yeeeeaaahhhh," growled Dewey, "'cause sometimes, there just ain't no girls around…"

I could take no more.

"Look fellas, you got the wrong idea. I mean, I'm just here for Mr. Harper. I mean, I'm not like that. I mean—"

They both started laughing.

"Oh, stop babblin'," said Ned, "Dewey's just having a little fun. He's seen *Deliverance* one too many times, if it ain't obvious."

Dewey squealed like a pig and they both snorted. I was so relieved that I polished off the beer, only to find another one in my hand. My head was starting to swim.

"So, what do you think of ol' Henry?" asked Ned. "He's a legend 'round here."

"He's fascinating," I said. "Who is this Joe he's always talking about?"

The two looked at each other.

"Well, Joe's a bigger celebrity around these parts than Henry, wouldn't you say, Dewey?"

"Bigger. Yeah."

"That's hard to believe," I said.

"Maybe harder to believe than you think, professor," said Ned and they both laughed again.

"Why's that?"

"Well, *professor*," said Dewey, grinning, "that's because Old Stinky Joe is a BIIIIGFOOOOOOT!" Somehow, he retained his smirk while snarling and holding his hands in front of him like they were claws.

It suddenly occurred to me what that shadowy figure was in Henry's painting, and that my research here might be for nothing.

They watched my reaction as I sank into doubt.

"Well, professor, you ain't any fun no more." Dewey jumped to his feet, and the next thing I knew, they were slipping out the door, Ned leaned in one last time.

"Sleep tight, Professor."

ALL OF THIS had a cumulative effect on me. Even with several beers, I had trouble falling asleep. Between every sound outside that trailer making me jump and my congested sinuses, there was no real rest now. This whole endeavor was appearing more and more useless, the golden jewel laid in front of me revealing a ruinous flaw. Maybe the best war story I'd ever heard, tainted by a mythical hoax. I laid there staring at the painting, seeing the madness that goes with genius, the stacks of art now the ravings of a lunatic, a gentle maniac's manifesto. I had half a mind to just get in my car and take off, but the old man had so enraptured me. I would have felt bad, had I just left. I wanted to give it one more try. Surely, he'd give me something, something to show me that I was again the victim of a couple of pathological liars. I braved it the rest of the night.

When I wandered down to the cabin in the morning, Henry fed me instant oatmeal. We then settled on his back porch, as lovely a place to spend a misty morning as anywhere on Earth. I set out the recorder, a little electronic sacrifice to bona fides, a prayer for the universe to give me what I needed. But first, I had to tackle the hairy elephant in the room.

(Begin Segment 5)

DM: HENRY, I'M not going to beat around the bush. Is Old Stinky Joe a Bigfoot?

HH: [shakes his head and chuckles] Aya.

DM: And you've seen Bigfoot how many times?

HH: Oh hell, son, does it matter? I mean, a person says they see a Bigfoot, what's it matter to anyone if'n it's more'n once? None to the outside world, that's fer sure, and once ya seen a bigfoot, well, ya gotta figure that that's gonna alter your worldview enough to where it don't matter if you see one again. Joe likes a cuppa tea every once in a while, orange and black pekoe. I don't know how many cups of tea I've poured for him.

DM: So, you have tea.

HH: I ain't the first.

[an extended silence follows. I could feel that he didn't care if I believed him. I tried to play along.]

DM: So how big is he anyway? Eight feet? Nine?

HH: See now, there you go, just like the rest. He ain't a thing for measuring or qualifying. He ain't a thing for DNA tests. He ain't a thing to be reduced to a picture. Joe is a force of nature, the old wild. He is a child of the wind. The forces that Joe feels moving through the universe are forces of which you are completely unaware. If you want to understand Joe, then you got to understand that you ain't truly got a handle on reality at all…[pauses]…sayin' Joe's six-foot-two or nine-foot-eight is kinda like you calling me a Buddhist. Not entirely accurate, I'd say. I just happen to share a similar view of existence. I didn't grow up with those gods and those demons. I only understand them with my noggin. The things that resonate in my heart come from my experience with the Buddhists, the Baptists, this mountain we sit on, and the things that life continues to give to me, like you. I hoped you was the one who would tell my story like it deserves to be told. I hoped that you could understand a moment in history as the dance of two spirits because that's the only way it can really be understood. Maybe you do and maybe you don't, and maybe you don't want to.

DM: It's all very subjective.

HH: Life is pretty subjective, wouldn't ya say?

[there is another extended silence, then a sound, barely audible on the recording, but which I can assure you was quite loud, like a large log snapping in the woods]

DM: What was *that*?

HH: Hmm? [Henry seemed distracted]

DM: That noise. It sounded big.

HH: Whereabouts, son?

DM: Up that hill. There! Did you hear that one? It must be a bear.

HH: I heard somethin'…[Henry sticks his nose in the air and starts sniffing—sniffing! Then he smiles broadly, looking over at me]…well, isn't this fortunate! [claps his hands together] Yes! Maybe I was wrong about you after all. You wait here. I'm going to go put on the kettle.

(End Segment 5)

THE ONLY FURTHER noises on the recorder are the thumpings, huffings, and muffled bumps as I grabbed the device and ran for the car. I was in a blind panic, I suppose from lack of rest. I was not acting rationally. As I turned the car around, Henry came out on the front porch. "Don't go!" he yelled. Off to my left and up the hill past the trailer, two small trees parted from each other at their tops, as if I were in the middle of some dinosaur movie. I floored it, fishtailing out of there in a cloud of dust with Henry Harper yelling, "He don't show up for just anyone!"

I didn't slow down until I was back at the Motel 6. After some long moments of limbs shaking and teeth chattering, I fell into floral-bedspread insensibleness for a couple hours, and then got up and began writing to you.

My best guess? Those devils, Dewey, and Ned, tumbled from the woods laughing as soon as I was out of sight. But since then, I have searched my actions over and over, and can't decide if I am proud or ashamed. I mean, if it was them, then why was I so frightened? Surely, I do not harbor even a tiny suspicion that there is such a thing as a Bigfoot (and I'd really appreciate it if this last part didn't get around the department) but I ran. I ran.

There is a dream that I have, a dream where I *dream* my father is about to die. In real life, I don't remember anything about Father dying. I was only four. In the dream, I'm four too, *dreaming* about my father dying that isn't dead yet, and then waking up, running to tell Mother. In the dream, Mother tells me that I couldn't have had that *dream*, because Father has died in real life and that I am just confused. When I begin to cry, she hands me a tablet for practicing writing the alphabet and tells me to do my ABCs.

I always wake from this with the urge to run for Daddy's room, before I realize he died a long time ago. And then, I feel what I can only describe as an echo. This is sort of how I felt today when I fled from Henry Harper's place. I suppose it doesn't matter. Here, in a few moments, before I hit the send button, I'll highlight these last few paragraphs and hit backspace.

Wish I had more here. Still, I am always interested in your opinion. Maybe if we just lost the crazy parts I could use it for my POW research or, possibly, we could publish it. Probably not, I know, but it's a hell of a story. I, of course, defer to your learned judgment.

Tomorrow, I head for Bluefield for my meeting with Seaman David Foster. Hoping for a productive interview there. Keep your fingers crossed that he doesn't believe in mermaids.

Your humble thesis slave,
Desmond

Bones

*"And this land is full of these little graves in the valleys, plains, and hills.
There's an angel, too, for each little grave an angel procession fills.
I know not how but I sometimes think that they lead us with gentle hand
And a whisper falls on a willing ear from the shore of a far-off land."*
— *"Grave on the Green Hillside," Aldine S. Kieffer*

H E DOESN'T KNOW her, this old woman, but she is here again. She is here again, and she wants to speak to him, he can tell. Her mouth moves. She gestures. She has something to impart. Bob Quinn sits on the edge of his parents' old bed in anchor pajamas, his unslippered feet resting on a woven oval area rug, mostly brown, on the wood floor. He can hear nothing but the hum and whoosh of the oil furnace kicking on. The woman's look turns to confusion, then frustration. She ceases moving her lips as if she knows there is no sound. This always happens. Every time she speaks words he cannot hear.

For two weeks now, he has been seeing her, and how odd that it happens here in his house and not the graveyards, where ghosts should be. He wonders if she could be an ancestor, but he knows that his paternal grandfather built this house and this woman resembles none of the family pictures. His impression of her clothes is old-fashioned, but somehow he can never see them clearly, always drawn to the uncertainty in the woman's eyes, always shattered to the bone for her failure to communicate. She is not at rest. She needs his help somehow.

It feels like an agreement of sorts, a justification of his work. Perhaps her mortal remains are in jeopardy. Maybe he can discover who she is and fight to protect her resting place before it is gone forever. And maybe on that day, she will appear to him no more. It fits, but then again, this is Bob's first ghost.

He reaches for his cell phone and she is gone. He doesn't understand why he never thinks of taking the picture first.

HE BOUNCES UP and down and back and forth in the driver seat. He shouldn't be taking the Caravan out this road. It's a 1998, falling apart. Bob imagines pieces of the minivan strewn behind him as he weaves around rocks and ruts, wincing in sympathetic pain at every hard drop-off. A mile out, the road turns into dried river bed, green with scrub weeds and hearty grasses, and he realizes there will be no other traffic. He stops the Dodge in a spot where it looks like he'll be able to turn around and gets out, proceeding on foot the rest of the way.

He doesn't know if there is anything out here. He has come on the word of an elderly woman from his church, Rosie McNaughton, who said she remembered a graveyard out this way, said her granddaddy called it the Pratt Cemetery, though she'd never known any Pratts personally, only Peters and Pringles. Bob has spent the last several days researching the Pratt family name, going to the library and the courthouse, and searching online. The only surviving family members are in Florida now and sold their land to American Coal years ago.

Technically, he is trespassing, but he knows that, sometimes, lines have to be crossed. As of tomorrow, he has the Burke kid for a month, so he needs to do this now. It wouldn't do to break the law in front of a kid serving his community service sentence.

The way is mostly uphill, and forty-eight-year-old Bob is soon breathing hard. The uneven terrain challenges his game leg, requiring more effort than normal. His mouth, already in a perpetual frown from his overbite, draws tighter as the physical effort increases. Beads of sweat pop from his forehead and flow like irrigation into his failing crop of hair. It is hot for early October, but the weather hasn't been right for years now, and Bob understands about global warming. It is one of those things he's learned along the way. There are a lot of things he's learned along the way. One thing about being an activist is that you end up talking to a lot of other activists. He stops to rest, unconsciously rubbing his fingers over the small bunch of cotton fabric in his pocket—a binkie, of sorts.

He wasn't always an activist, and at one point even worked for Delphi Coal, but that was before they tried to cheat him from his Worker's Comp and Disability when he was injured. Then a different company out of Kentucky, Murphy Energy, made the last years of Mama's life a living hell when they bought the land that held her family cemetery. That whole experience had changed how he saw the industry forever. What he'd learned since had changed how he saw companies in general.

Further on the dilapidated road, he spies an opening beyond the trees to his right, an area of grass and saplings which looks to have once been a path. He works his way through the rocks and brush carefully. Hot days, late in fall, bring the snakes out to sun on the rocks. He reaches the clearing and looks around at the thigh–high wheat grass, still clinging to a pale remnant of green, giving way to brown. Some of the dead stalks are already bent over, fatally creased, ready to be vanquished by the first snow. The rest of the small meadow remains defiant.

To his left, he sees the telltale form of carved stone, its arched countenance visible through the thinning weeds. Now, looking at the size of the area, he wishes he would have brought a sickle. He approaches the stone and clears the grass around it. The marker stands about a foot and a half high and an inch and a half thick. Dark gray lichen swirls over its face in a fractal pattern, casting doubt about the stone's original color.

Quinn pulls a can of shaving cream from his backpack. He wipes a generous portion across the face of the stone and uses a rag to clean off the excess, leaving only the inscription filled with the white foam.

Daniel Evans Pratt
b. 1801 d. 1857

The shaving cream will not harm the stone and will wash off in the next rain. He writes the name and dates in a notebook, then stands and looks around. This is going to take a while. He begins kicking through the weeds, keeping a sharp eye for stones set flush with the ground and even broken pieces. He begins to hum an old bluegrass gospel song, and eventually, the words spring from him in high nasal tones: "How peaceful the slumber, how happy the waking, where death is only a dream."

He moves through the brush, stooped, clearing out the weeds to expose the stones and, as the sun crests above him, Bob Quinn sings to the dead.

"A LOT OF people don't realize how long bones last," he says. "Yes," the clerk at the convenience store says, "that's interesting."

AT HOME, HE sits at his computer and opens his notebook. He transfers the names he was able to recover from the stones, etching them into silicon, into a data file titled, "Pratt Family Cemetery." If he can prove someone noteworthy is buried there, he can apply to the West Virginia Historical Preservation Society for protected status. Too many of these old family graveyards are gone across the state, across the country.

The family cemetery issue came to his attention when the blasting began on Spenser Mountain and he overheard Jim Perkins at church, talking to a group of parishioners about how the Walker Family Cemetery was being turned under. The thought had shocked him. The bones of all those folks, all that history, lost, scattered, buried deep under landfill by those who would have everyone forget the past—and the future—if they had their way.

Then, after what happened to Mama, and what she had to go through to get that company to relocate those graves, all the while crying at night wondering if her kin would be there for the resurrection, well, he sees now. He didn't always. The thought of such desecration still offends him, more even than it did when he first heard of the Walker cemetery, scattered to the wind and folded into the earth.

He adds the Pratt Family Cemetery file to his pending research folder.

Bob turns his attention to the blinking light on his home phone sitting on the hutch next to the kitchen doorway. Three messages. Two of them are from the Charleston Medical Center Department of Oncology, one is from the county prosecutor's office. He erases the hospital messages before the woman's voice can remind him that he needs to schedule his follow-up appointment. He listens to the third message. "Mr. Quinn, this is Margie at the prosecutor's office. I'm just calling to remind you that Mr. Burke is scheduled to begin his community service with you tomorrow. Hopefully, by now, you've gotten the forms in the mail. Just fill those out as you go along and mail them back when the thirty days are over, and please, let us know immediately if Mr. Burke does not report for work. Thank you and call if you have any questions."

Tomorrow.

He walks into the kitchen, an addition to the back of his grandparents' two-story, box-structure farmhouse. He lived here with Mama for eighteen years, first working as an electrician for Delphi, before the transformer explosion crippled his leg, and then taking care of her and the house as she was less and less able. When she died a few years back, he stayed in the house alone. He keeps everything exactly as she left it.

The forms from the county are lying on the faded blue tablecloth that covers the kitchen table, painted off-white. They are unfolded and lie partially concealing the unopened envelope from the hospital laboratory that contains his test results. He thinks about his phone conversation with the

Burke kid, already with an attitude before the job has even started. Bob isn't looking forward to this. He feels a knot in his stomach. The kid is a bad element. Everyone in town knows that. Bob microwaves a frozen meat loaf and takes it back to the living room, where he eats on a tray in front of the television.

He cleans his mess in the scarred, white kitchen sink and returns to the computer where he checks his email and logs on to the cemetery preservation chat group. He occupies the rest of his time before bed doing searches on some of the names found earlier in the day. None of them are noteworthy, it seems. It angers him, what constitutes noteworthy. The lack of respect. And then, there are punks like Dewey Burke, who get a kick out of knocking over headstones.

As Bob readies himself for bed, he wonders, would anyone think his Grandpappy Wilson, or his daddy even, were noteworthy? Or him?

GRANDPAPPY WILSON'S FUNERAL was held at the Vernon Funeral Home in Trevelton and he was buried on family land. After the service, friends and kin gathered at the home of his sister Mae, a farmhouse a few miles out of town. Family came from all around Bergen County and beyond: Parkersburg, Richmond, Cincinnati. They filled the house.

Young Bobby Quinn, just seven years old, was fawned over by relatives he didn't even know, and dragged out to play with cousins upon cousins in the great yard. It was a kind of paradise for an awkward late-arrival like Bobby. His older brother and sister were married and moved out by this time, and Daddy had begun to slow down. He would be gone in ten years' time. Everybody told Bobby's mama what a miracle he was, to which she wearily agreed. But miracles, being so few, are lonely things.

Every surface of Aunt Mae's house was decorated with covered dishes: corn on the cob, fresh sliced tomatoes and cucumbers, breads, homemade jellies and jams, cookies and cobblers, pastries, pies, and cakes. All through the day, as relatives caught up with each others' lives, on the porch, in the kitchen, around the living room and the great dining room table, the joys of family were celebrated. Bobby had barely known his grandpappy but thought he must have been a truly great man for so many to have loved him. Rather than a moment of sadness, it solidified in the young boy's memory as a moment of perfection, and the funeral, to Bobby Quinn, became a place of strange joy.

"HELLO, MR. QUINN," Senator Greenback's secretary says, the enthusiasm of her phone salutation dropping off a cliff. "I'm afraid the Senator is in meetings all morning. Can I help you?"

"I'm just calling to check on the status of Bill 223-B, Lucy. Has the Senator said anything about it?"

"No, Mr. Quinn, I haven't heard a thing, sorry."

"It's important that we get that bill out of committee and onto the floor this session. Has the Senator spoken with any of the committee members yet?" Bob paces the living room as he speaks into the wireless handset, up and down in front of the fireplace mantle, then across in front of the hutch. Adjusting items in both locations each time he passes. A family photograph, taken in the late sixties.

"Mr. Quinn, the legislative session doesn't begin for nearly four months, so I think it's hardly an issue yet."

"I disagree, Lucy. These restrictions need to be applied soon. All it takes is the mineral rights and these people could mount a drilling rig right next to my mother's grave."

A small blue porcelain ballerina.

"Yes sir—"

Bob is noticing that he needs to dust. He puffs himself up. There is a need to display some authority here.

"The coal company has to respect these limits. State government has to respect these limits. For Pete's sake, even hunters have to abide by the five-hundred-foot distance. Why are we having such a problem applying them to the gas industry?"

"I don't know, Mr. Quinn—"

He straightens a stack of envelopes on the hutch.

"Would you want to visit your mother's grave next to a drilling rig?"

"My mother's not dead, Mr. Quinn."

"That's hardly the point, Lucy, now is it?"

She sighs as Bob turns a picture of his maternal grandparents slightly to the left. "I suppose not, Mr. Quinn."

"And has the Senator said anything about the family cemetery legislation idea I talked to him about?"

"No sir, he hasn't."

"Not said anything about writing it and having you type it up for the next session?"

He fiddles with the latch on the door of the old wind-up clock on the mantle, casually checks through the glass to see if the key is still inside.

"No, sir."

"When will he be in?"

"Oh," she pauses, "he's in meetings all day. And I think he's traveling tomorrow. I'm not sure."

He stops at the hutch and grabs a pen and paper.

"Will he be here in his district?"

"Honestly, Mr. Quinn, I just don't know at the moment. My appointment book seems to be missing."

"Can I leave a message for him?"

"I already have your inquiries written down for him, Mr. Quinn. Is there anything else?"

He is dismissed from the halls of democracy. He puts down the pen and paper, hangs up and stares at the phone in his hand. He jumps as it rings while he's looking at it. There is laughter behind him. Charleston Medical Center. He puts the wireless unit back in its cradle without answering. He turns and flinches when he sees the old woman across the room, standing right next to where Dewey Burke sits on the couch. She is trying to speak and failing again.

The kid does not appear to see the ghost. Bob closes his mouth quickly.

"So," Burke says, "This is what you *do*, huh?"

"WHAT DO THEY pay you for this?" asks the Burke kid. He is raking the leaves and branches from between headstones. Bob pulls the last of the weeds from around the stones. This will be his last round of cleanups for the season.

"I don't get paid," he says, "Maintenance on these private cemeteries isn't covered in the county budget. This is volunteer work."

"So, all these people got you doin' their work for 'em for free." He laughs. "Sucker."

"The county owns some of these. The state. Some are still owned by the mining companies, and some owners don't live around here no more. So there's nobody else. Just me, and for the next thirty days, you."

"How many of these are there? I only knew about Sunny Hills and the one by the church."

"The one you desecrated?"

Burke doesn't answer.

"Why would anyone do that? Knock over headstones."

The Burke kid continues to rake and then says, "Ya know," a pause. "It's my personal opinion that this here place would be a sight prettier with the leaves still layin' about."

"We're going to rake them up anyway."

"Whatever you say, Mr. Quinn." He sings it, the flannel-clad shit.

This is not starting well. The kid's been a smart-ass the entire day. Twenty-nine more days of this. He must get hold of it now.

"Those headstones you knocked over were someone's relatives, someone's grandparents, great-grandparents. Would you want someone to do that to *your* grandparent's grave?"

"Seein' as how I ain't never met a grandparent once, I guess I just couldn't give a fuck. So, spare me your fake outrage, *Mr. Quinn.*"

Other than by the coal company, Quinn has never, in his entire life, been called a fake. He pulls weeds as if he's ripping Burke's head from his shoulders.

"You know, I'm thinking more and more like I might need to call the prosecutor's office and cancel this whole thing if I don't start getting a little respect here."

"Yes sir, *Mr. Quinn.*"

Quinn stops yanking native flora, sighs, then says, "Maybe you call me Bob."

"*Bob.*"

"Well, not when you say it like that."

Twenty-nine more days.

"YOU KNOW, EVEN after cremation there's still bone fragments left," he says to Mrs. Collins at the county courthouse in Trevelton.

"Even after cremation," she says. "I'll be."

DADDY'S DEATH WAS the first time Bob felt profound sadness at a funeral, the first time he cried, the first time he'd really pondered eternal absence. When the preacher had finished and most of the family had already walked away, Mama stood by the coffin as it was lowered and sang "See That My Grave is Kept Green." She sobbed between verses, sometimes between words. She couldn't finish.

At home, the family gathering paled to those of the past. There wasn't as much food. There were fewer kin. Bobby was too old now for playing in the yard, and he was awkward with these few cousins who were strangers to him. At his first opportunity, he stole out the back door and sequestered himself in the garage.

The side door of the garage opened behind him just as he was finding his solitary sorrow, head in palms. His cousin, Hattie, slipped inside, looking over her shoulder. At sixteen, Hattie had changed from the last time he saw her, and seventeen-year-old Bob found himself uncomfortable in her gaze.

"You okay in here?"

"Yeah."

"Sorry about your dad, I mean, Uncle Frank." She walked over to where the push mower sat in the corner and ran her hand along the push bar.

"Yeah."

She sat down next to him on the wooden bench, once painted red, now flecked dark red and gray.

"So," she said, "how have you been—I mean, other than today?"

"Alright, I guess."

"You gotcha a girl?"

"No." He looked away from her. She had on a knee-length light-blue dress. She was dark haired with a wide nose and full lips, an Eastern-European sort of beauty.

"What!" she said. "I don't believe it."

"Don't make fun."

"I'm not making fun. Just don't believe it, is all." She reached above her head and pulled tentatively at a coil of rope that hung from a nail.

"I'm not what you'd call a prize, Hattie."

"Aw, it ain't all on the outside, Bobby. And you ain't all that bad."

He kept looking at his father's workspace. Screwdrivers in their proper slots, hammers of all sorts, a power drill. His left hand gripped the edge of the bench with the strength of the desperate. Hattie stayed quiet for a few seconds and then stood, touching him on the shoulder and turning in front of him. "I tell you what," she said. She slipped the straps of her dress over her shoulders and let it slide down her body, gingerly stepping out of it and draping it over the front of the car.

"Hattie Wilson! Put your dress back on!" Bob looked around in panic, trying not to stare at her. Her bra and panties fell to the floor and she stepped toward him.

"Hattie! We're cousins! Cousins aren't supposed to—"

She reached down and took his hand and put it on her round, perfect breast.

"Mutant babies." His voice had already mutated.

"We're second cousins, silly. *That's* okay." She began moving his hand down her belly. "And ain't gonna be no babies." She leaned down and whispered, "I'm on the pill. Don't tell Mama."

Bob couldn't take his eyes off her now.

"Go ahead," she said, "stick a finger in there."

"IF THE REMAINS have been disturbed, how will they rise for the resurrection?"

Reverend Mooney gives him a thin-lipped, sympathetic smile, his head tilted slightly. "You're doing God's work, Robert," he says.

THE NEXT MORNING, Quinn tells Burke to wait in the van and makes a quick stop at the Sunny Hills Cemetery where he drops off a thousand-dollar check to the caretaker, all that is left on his balance. His plot is secure.

As he's pulling out, the Burke kid says, "Phew, I was thinking we had to clean that whole place. Scared me for a second."

"No, I just had some business to take care of."

"Oh yeah? What kinda business?"

"Nothin' for you to concern yourself about."

"No seriously, y'all got some kinda secret society of weird graveyard guys or somethin'?"

Quinn doesn't answer. The radio isn't on.

Burke is mercifully quiet for about a mile down the road. And then, "Did you ever wonder what it'd be like to fuck a corpse, Bob?"

Bob swerves the car off the road and slides to a stop. He turns to yell at the kid only to see him bent in laughter.

"Damn, Bob, you really need to learn to take a joke."

"That wasn't funny."

"Was for me."

Quinn pulls the minivan back out onto the road.

"You're a strange bird, Bob."

Twenty-eight more days.

"THE COAL COMPANIES are stealing our heritage right out from under us," he says, fingering the worn fabric in his pocket.

The woman in the Walmart parking lot edges her buggy away, nodding with a friendly smile. "It was nice to meet you," she says.

THE PARKER CEMETERY is their seventh stop in as many days.

"So, you never did tell me how many of these little pissant graveyards there are." Burke toys with the rake.

"Twenty-one in Bergen County that we know about. Twenty-two if you count the Pratt cemetery I found a week ago."

"You go lookin' for em, too? Holy shit."

"Bring the rake and stuff from the back."

Quinn uses a kneeling support to get down and pull the weeds; otherwise he wouldn't be able to get up easily. His leg hurts. He should make the kid weed, but they are especially sick of each other today, and he doesn't want to disturb the dead with an argument.

He kneels in front of a stone marked, "Winnifred Parker, 1873-1921." He hums because he is self-conscious about singing and that makes him feel guilty. Then, as he pulls out a clump of goldenrod, something tickles his thigh.

"What's this hanging out of old Bob's pocket?"

Quinn turns and sees him holding a pair of panties aloft. His mind bounces around like it's in a pinball machine. To the moment when Hattie, back in her dress, pressed them into his palm with the words, "Something to remember me by." To six years later, when he'd heard she died of an overdose, and sobbed into them every night for months. He reaches for the panties, but the Burke kid pulls them back.

"I didn't know, Bob!" he says. "I did not know that you had a thing for the ladies underwear."

Before Quinn can react, the kid pulls out a cell phone and aims it at him, holding the panties up in the foreground. Bob stands there, unable to act, as the device beeps.

Burke puts the phone back in his pocket and begins examining the panties. Turning them around, mock-sniffing them.

"I've been wondering what you had in that pocket that you had to touch all the time. I was beginning to think you was some kind of pervert." Burke turns them around and around, scrutinizing. "I wasn't too far from the truth there, eh, Bob? What is it? You like to wear 'em? Look at yourself in the mirror? Do they make you think of little girls?"

First a fake, now a transvestite and child molester. Bob screams and leaps for the kid. He grabs at the panties, but the kid yanks them away. Bob's momentum carries him forward, pushing Burke backward against a stone. The marker falls over and hits the ground a half-second before the kid does, breaking in two. Burke's eyes are wide and he is laughing. Quinn stands above him, quaking, horrified, his desperation gathering in the corner of his eyes.

"Give 'em back!"

The kid scrambles backward, away from Quinn, and jumps to his feet.

"Here's how I see it, Bob. I'm gonna finish out the day for ya here…and then, I think my community service is done. If you don't want everyone knowing that you assaulted me, or that you carry ladies underwear in your pocket, then you'll just go ahead and fill those forms out here in a couple weeks like I finished my service with flying colors. That sound okay to you?"

Bob can see nothing but his shame and heartbreak flapping in the breeze. He nods silently, his hand stretched out in front of him, his eyes begging.

"I think I'll keep em," says Burke.

"No, please."

Burke scrutinizes him, rolls his eyes, and tosses the underwear back. "Here's your panties, Bob." He grabs his rake and resumes clearing leaves and branches and they work the next few hours in silence. Every once in a while, the kid emits a malicious chuckle.

BOB STANDS AT Mama and Daddy's graves and tells them that he will just be a few rows down. He thinks about Mama, standing here singing, and wonders who will keep his grave green. Who will sing? No one, he supposes.

Everything used to seem so permanent: family, mountains, graves. Now it's all slipping away into some black hole. He looks around the cemetery at the few stubborn clover blooms, recalling that it was another year without bees. Bees. What could be more eternal than bees? The graveyards used to be alive with them, and now they rarely cross his gaze. He'd read of entire colonies never finding their way home, set upon by marauders, decimated by mites that eat them from the inside out. Bob suspects everything is being eaten from the inside out.

At home, he worries. Does the whole town know his secret? The whole world? Would everyone be laughing at him more than they already do? He deletes his phone messages, searches tombstone names until his head nods, and goes to bed.

HE IS AWAKENED in the middle of the night from a dream that he cannot recall. In the dark, he sees the old woman again across the room. He starts, sitting up in bed, throwing his legs over the side. His rush of surprise does not last long.

"What do you want from me?" he asks.

Again, the mouth opens and no sound emerges. Again, the furrowed brow, the frustrated façade. Again, with the thoughts of the day still in the front of his mind, he wonders.

What is she trying to tell him? Is she telling him that there *is* something permanent? Or is she telling him nothing is? Why is she here?

This time, he doesn't reach for the cell phone to take a picture. Instead, in the quiet of the hundred-year-old home, in the dark of night, Bob Quinn clears his throat, rubs his eyes, and begins to softly sing "Grave on the Green Hillside." His mind is filled with recurring images of Dewey Burke holding Hattie's underwear and laughing. As much as he wants to hate Burke for mocking his life's tragedy, he can't get over the feeling that he envies the kid his freedom from caring. Bob wonders briefly if he is afraid of not dying.

He looks back up to see her smiling, a peaceful smile, a loving smile like his mother would give him, a smile that contains both weariness and contentment. He has the overwhelming impression that her grave is already gone and it doesn't matter. One thing about the smile seems obvious to him. She wants him to live.

He hangs his head again and takes a deep breath, absently examining the anchor design on his pajamas, trying to find the part of himself that wants that, too. When he looks up again, she is gone. He gets out of bed and walks across the bedroom toward the stairs. The October night rises through the floorboards and chills him to his bones. Downstairs, an envelope waits in the dark, like the future.

Blood

THE SOUND OF his wife's shriek from the backyard vibrated through the aluminum and plywood walls of the double-wide, across the floor, through the brown faux-leather of the La-Z-Boy, and up Jack Foster's spine, where it rattled his teeth and shook his brain loose from an afternoon airing of *The People's Court*. He turned the volume down and waited, frowning.

"JAAAAACK!"

He slammed his can of Milwaukee's Best, shallow and warm with backwash, onto the end table, an announcement to the empty trailer. He pulled himself from the chair with a grunt and a mumble. "Damn woman." Last he knew, Annie Mae was hanging laundry. It was hard to tell what she needed.

Ever, really.

He heard the snarls and screams as soon as he opened the back door and started down the wooden steps. The stair structure, open, with a thin iron framework, rocked slightly as he descended. Annie Mae must have heard him.

"Get out here!" she yelled. "Peppy's got that damn groundhog!"

Halfway down the steps, Jack paused and thought about going back for his rifle. As he considered the idea, the boys emerged from the corner of his vision, running down from the woods. Earlier, Ned had burst in the front door asking for a hammer and nails. He and Dewey Burke from up the road were trying to build a fort out of sticks and logs. No way, Jack told him. The kid had no sense of what things cost. The notion prompted him to leave the gun behind. Ammo was way more expensive than nails.

Let the dog earn its keep. If he'd known how much it would cost to feed the thing, he wouldn't have brought it home for Christmas whatever year that was, three, four back. It seemed like a good idea at the time. A free gift for the kid. Now just a pain in the ass for Jack. It hadn't taken long, after he hurt his back and went on disability, to put the dog outside for good. He wasn't put on this earth to cater to a dog that always expected something, accusing him with its eyes. The kid cried himself to sleep for weeks after that, and the fucking dog whined and howled.

Jack pushed through the line of hanging linen, where Annie Mae stood some five feet away from the clash of tooth and claw, urging the dog on.

The shed, like the trailer, sat elevated on concrete blocks for the times the creek flooded. The dog had the woodchuck by the back foot, trying to prevent it from getting under there, but that was like having a snake by the tail. The rodent kept twisting and biting as if it were made of something other than bone, bringing blood to the dog's hip and leg. Blood streamed from the groundhog's foot as well, but the appendage wasn't useless yet. The groundhog spun again, folding itself in half to open another wound in the dog's side with its vicious front teeth, staining another spot of the golden fur red. The dog yelped, jumped back, and then dove after the wounded foot again.

The boys stopped behind Jack, breathing hard, eyes wide. He glanced at them in time to see his son's anticipation turn to panic. No surprise there. As he'd figured out long ago, the eight-year-old was a pussy.

Annie screamed, "Get it, Peppy! Get it!" Dewey cheered with her and Jack laughed. Ned stood there, limp.

The woodchuck lunged for the shed again, but its foot was broken and the thrust was crooked. That was all the dog needed to get on top of the squirming animal, and her mouth nearly vanished into the varmint's neck. Peppy had it now, pinned down, squeezing the air and blood out of the beast. It jerked wildly every ten seconds or so, and the dog clamped down harder, trying to shake it, a futile attempt to break its neck. Soon, the struggles came less frequently. The rodent's eyes went dead before its breathing, or the jerking, stopped.

The battle over, Jack's eyes fell to the boys. Dewey's expression was hard to judge, excited, but conflicted. His eyes kept moving between his best friend and the dead groundhog, his exhilaration retreating. Ned stood there, his mouth open, his eyes shedding silent tears like those weird-ass times when he was an infant, when the tears would just flow, his tiny mouth open but with no sound, and Jack would wonder if the kid had gone mute. Annie used to cry too when that happened. She said the baby could see his own fate, whatever the fuck that meant.

Well, there you go, he thought. This'll help make a man of him, show him how the world really is.

He turned back toward the trailer, taking one last look behind him. Annie was praising the bloody dog which was limping, and Jack supposed she might be hurt pretty good. Peppy attempted to shake the dead groundhog like an oversized toy, but the carcass was too heavy and all the mutt could do was drag it around as she hobbled backwards in a circle, tossing her head back and forth.

Tears still coursed over the boy's reddened cheeks. Ned looked at his father, his eyes tightened into an accusation. It should have earned him a thrashing, that look, but Jack had better things to do today than whip an insolent kid. He turned his attention to the trailer, his mind set on another cold one and television justice.

The Moth in the Stair

ETTA BOONE STEPPED onto her back porch to the sound of voices from the neighboring hillside. Being unaccustomed to human noises so early, she cupped her hands around her coffee mug and strained to hear the spirited conversation through the morning mist. A line of trees in her backyard blocked her view, a mix of evergreen and deciduous species thick with late spring foliage, and she couldn't imagine who might be arguing on that particular hillside at this hour of the morning. Earlier, she'd heard Tim Martz drive out for work, and it would be a half hour before the Martz kids clamored down the road toward the turnaround where the school bus would pick them up. It would be especially unusual, she thought, for it to be the Smiths who lived a little further on down the hollow.

Surely, they were arguing, louder now, whoever they were, and she leaned over her wood porch rail, tugging at the sounds with her ears, willing them to make sense. Was that an "at"? Was there a "Jack"? Did she know any Jacks?

The flock of water fowl burst out low over the treetops in front of her like a honking blitzkrieg coming in under the radar. Etta flinched, spilling coffee as she stepped back, inhaling harshly as if in imitation of the barking mallards flying low above her.

Recovering her wits, she watched the last of the V fly past overhead and listened to the argument fade away on the other side of the house.

Startled by ducks. She shook her head as her breathing slowed.

Still, she found herself cocking an ear toward the hillside. She'd been so certain it was bickering. Now, there was nothing but the morning birds, the occasional buzz of an early fly, and the wispy cotton sound of the fog creeping slowly across the yard, whispering the world to sleep for just a little bit longer.

She walked to the far end of the porch, opened the wooden bin that was secured to the railing and, using a plastic flour scoop, shoveled birdseed from the bag inside to the feeder that hung on a shepherd's hook planted just outside her kitchen window. When she finished, she sat down in the camping chair that she'd bought at Walmart and waited for the chickadee who always braved her presence first. She used to sit on the swing in the mornings, but these days, it was just too hard for her bony behind, even with the cushion. The camping chair was a little harder to extricate herself from, but for her morning coffee, she preferred the comfort. And what was coffee for, if not for getting out of chairs?

This was Etta's time of the day, when the world belonged to her alone, and sometimes, she would sit out here in the early hours and watch the ghosts of children play, ducking in and out of the grape arbor, swinging on the tire that no longer hung from a high branch on the walnut tree down near the garage. For years, a fragment of the rope, knotted and frayed, had clung to the branch, strands dancing in the breeze, but now even that was gone. Often, she would sip her brew and remember Frank, working in the garden or emerging from the garage, in either case dirty, and ready to be intercepted before he tracked up her clean floors.

Today, her thoughts remained fixed on the ducks. How was it that some things could just turn into something else, all of a sudden, just like that? The morning felt off kilter, and the waterfowl put her in mind of her drive to Trevelton just the day before to deposit her Social Security check and pay her property taxes. Driving past the first dwellings at the edge of town, she had stepped on the brakes to avoid a scurrying chipmunk, only to see it change into a leaf, pushed along the road by the wind. The driver behind her laid on his horn.

At the courthouse, an out-of-order sign hung on the elevator. Etta braced herself and climbed the stairs to the third-floor tax office, stopping briefly at each landing to collect herself. On the second-floor landing, she saw the most beautiful gray moth, motionless and flattened to the stair like a perfectly mounted and framed butterfly. She leaned down for a better look, but it receded into the pattern of the marble as she drew close.

Thinking now about the three occurrences together, it seemed to her a disturbing pattern, an omen of the sort her Granny Prescott had spoken when she was a child. "A sparrow in the house is death," she said. Things could change on you just like that, into other, terrible things. She flailed for a better thought. Maybe God was speaking to her. Maybe He was showing her that it was possible to become something else, that maybe you could do it all over again differently.

She thought a lot about doing things over.

ETTA HAULED THE stepstool from the pantry and set it up in front of her sink, careful to straddle the soft spot in the kitchen floor where the board needed replacing. She climbed to the top step, hanging onto the aluminum handle for support. Thursdays were cabinet dusting days, and from her hunched stance, she extended the elongated feather duster to the top of the painted cabinets and began dragging it across the top, one hand preserving her fragile balance.

The days all had their chores, a promise she had made to herself when Frank had passed on ten years ago. Mondays were for tending to the outside. Tuesdays, she dusted the living room and dining room, pulling out the china, wiping it, and replacing it in the cabinet. Wednesdays, she changed linens and dusted the connected upstairs bedrooms. Fridays were for sweeping and vacuuming, and Saturday was for the wash. But Thursdays were for the cabinets and the refrigerator and the old baking cupboard with its trinkets. She stretched perilously from the top of the stool to reach the ends of the cupboards, her "dance with disaster," she called it, when she had a mind to talk out loud to the spirits of the house.

There were no chores on Sunday. Sunday was the Lord's Day, though she didn't know what that meant anymore. Maybe she had never really known, but it's what she'd been taught growing up and the idea stuck, stubborn as thistle.

It was at a church social in 1951 that Franklin Boone had asked Etta to dance and she had first found his crooked nose cute. She was so fascinated by how his large hands enveloped hers completely, captivated by their immensity on the small of her back. The year before, he had dropped out of school to work as a mechanic for Chickasaw Logging, and she had forgotten about him until that night.

She wondered what might have happened had she waited on Terrence Rivers, the dark, attractive boy she'd been set on back then. He never approached her to dance, but she had been hoping he would until Franklin had swept her from her seat. Terrence moved away from Dogleg Bend after high school and she never heard tell of him again.

She married Franklin a year later. They bought their little house. Frank built his garage and started his business. Then along came Donny, and everything seemed fine. But sometimes, chipmunks changed into lifeless leaves, tossed by the wind.

Etta stepped down and moved the stepladder to the baking cabinet. She wondered where Terrence Rivers ended up and if he was still alive. In what exotic places might she have lived? What normal family might she have had?

ROBIN MARTZ STOPPED by around two thirty, long after Etta had finished her chores and eaten a tomato sandwich. Etta put on another pot of coffee and the two sat in her kitchen, watching the birds at her feeder.

"Etta, it worries me, you going up and down those stairs in there all the time. You ever thought of getting one of those chairlifts?"

"Oh honey, I could never afford something like that. I'm fine. Those stairs ain't beat me yet."

"Still, though," said Robin, "you over here all by yourself with no one to look after you."

"Well, I got you, now don't I?" Etta patted Robin's hand and smiled.

Etta counted young Robin and her husband Tim to be her only friends in the world. They'd moved here a couple years before from Ohio with their two kids when Tim got a drilling job with Appalachian Gas and Oil. Robin came over to introduce herself and they hit it off, two women who both needed someone to talk to.

The idea of being old and alone stunned Robin. She'd quizzed Etta about the family picture on her hutch, but short of learning that both the husband and son were deceased, she could never get any real information out of her, and there were no other pictures to compare it to. All Etta ever said was, "I ain't got no family no more. It don't matter the why or how or wherefore."

In no time at all, Robin and her husband became a help to her. Twice, they'd even driven her over to Trevelton and taken her out to dinner with their family.

"Oh, what a beautiful cardinal," Robin said, eyes toward the window.

"They's beautiful birds, alright," said Etta. She sighed, almost imperceptibly. "Seems a fine thing to fly around and make the world a prettier place."

Robin admired her, once again trying to fathom the pain behind the old woman's eyes as Etta smiled at the bird, distant.

"Oh shoot, Etta, I can't put this off. I gotta ask you a huge favor."

Etta laughed. "Well, I expect you better ask then. What is it, sweetie?"

"Truth is, Robby waited until last night before giving me a note from school about an end–of–the–year bake sale."

"You want I should make ya some of my cookies?"

"Oh, would you? Anything! Whatever is easiest for you. You're such a marvelous baker. You remember how those women ridiculed my baking. I'm still ostracized. I swear, you'd think I was the new kid in school."

Robin grimaced when she admitted that she needed them the next day and offered any help she could give. When she left, Etta could still hear her question echoing.

"Are you sure?"

Later, stirring her soup on the stove, she thought fondly of Robin and her family and how they made her feel like the grandmother she'd never gotten to be. Etta set the spoon down and glanced up through the sheer curtain on the kitchen door toward the Martz home, only the top of which was visible from here. Her breath hitched in her throat as smoke roiled and billowed over their roof. Etta ran for the door, pushed aside the curtain, and the rolling smoke turned into gray slate roofing tile, obscured by a shaggy pine bough bouncing in the wind.

SHE HAD ALREADY sifted the flour and sugar when she discovered she was nearly out of vanilla extract. It wouldn't do to call Robin, who would surely have none. Etta looked out the window at the fading day. She hated to drive after nightfall, but if she left immediately, she might have time. Etta gathered her pocketbook and umbrella. The wind was still blowing and the weatherman had said storms were moving in. Locking her door, she walked to the drive and started her old station wagon, turning it onto Tanners Road, a one-lane road pretending to be a two-lane road, like so many in West Virginia. After a few miles, she turned left onto Jackson Road, marginally better.

It was the turn onto Route Twelve she dreaded. The coal trucks were merciless. Luckily, there were none in sight when she turned left toward the Walmart, still another seven miles up the road. Already, she could see she wouldn't make it back before dark.

Storm clouds rolled in over the hills, bringing a violent darkness. The clouds were the color of bruised sky, streaked like a tornado that was rolling instead of dancing. It would be a toad strangler, as Papa used to say, like the one in 1984, the night after Donny drove the bus off one of the high turns on Kevin's Way.

She remembered the night Donny was conceived: Franklin sneaking into bed, freshly showered, gently slipping his giant hands around her and pulling her close. She'd known earlier that it was coming from the life in his eye. The memory slipped like a dream to Donny as an infant, then dissolved into his toddler image trying to walk in his father's boots that fit him like hip waders floating downstream, to his first day of school, to his Lone Ranger costume, to that time he'd been allowed to row the boat merrily out onto the lake, to the time Franklin had handed him the keys and said, "It's yours," then to plummeting like a cascading waterfall to the night his father first beat him for drinking. But that's where it often ended.

She hated this road.

In her rearview, the overzealous truck driver could not be seen, only his massive grill, ornamented with beast fangs and belligerent headlights. It would be this way for the next several miles, but she was afraid to go any faster.

She loved Franklin dearly, adored making love to him, but she wished she'd never let him touch her that night.

As she pulled into the Walmart, the coal truck made a show of passing her. Mercifully, she didn't have to walk the entire length of the store to get to the vanilla, but by the time she left the maze-like structure, darkness was upon her world, the first thick drops of rain spattering the pavement. The worst of the storm didn't hit until she made it safely off Route Twelve back onto Jackson Road, four miles or so from home. The lightning birthed stark and fleeting shadows, transient, morphing figures along the road, gone as quickly as they appeared. Etta crept by, bent over the wheel, trying to see through the glare and the liquid thick upon her windshield, agitated by two rubber strips ineffectively flipping back and forth.

The deer poked its head out into the road just as she was about to pass it, her headlamps already too far ahead to set the creature's eyes aglow. It startled her, and she turned to see it looking at her through the watery passenger window as she drove by. Too slowly, she applied the brake in fear of others. She came near to a dead stop before looking into her mirror to find that the deer had turned into a mailbox, a mailbox she'd passed a million times.

THE EYES, THOUGH. The eyes still preoccupied her.

At home, as she baked, she thought about them, beautiful dark globes, lashes holding water at their tips. She could have sworn they blinked at her as she drove past. She could have sworn it was chewing, its lower jaw moving side to side. It *was* a deer, if only for a moment.

The smoke, the deer, the voices from the hillside, the chipmunk. And the moth, such a beautiful thing. Were they all real for just a moment? The question preoccupied her to the point that she almost burned her first batch of cookies. She laid them on wax paper to cool, then arranged them in a Tupperware box that held four dozen or so. As the layers grew, she separated them with more wax paper. She set to filling it. She'd forgotten the purpose for her baking and wanted as many kids as possible to get a cookie.

Only one child remained on the bus with Donny when it went over the side of the mountain. She, too, was killed.

It was the next day when the storm had blown in. The police came to talk with Frank and Etta, and the long, slow change began. When told about the girl's state of dress, Etta responded with, "Well, I'm sorry, but I just can't believe our Donnie had anything to do with that." She didn't want to accept any of the speculation and neither did Frank, even as the knowledge spread and Frank's business dried up and they quit going to a church filled with hypocrites.

And now, she thought, waiting for the cookie timer, the Lord is showing me a different world. Perhaps, it was a world coming into being just for her, where a beautiful gray moth with opaque and delicately veined wings would rise up out of the marble, alight on the tip of her fingers, and she would be able to start anew.

By the time she loaded the last of the cookies into the Tupperware, it was past eleven-thirty. She made her way up the stairs to Donny's old bedroom, long since purged of any trace of him. The storm had moved on, but occasional flashes of far-flung blue light filled the darkened spaces. Passing through his room, the lightning flared once more, and there he stood in the corner. "I'm sorry Mama, so sorry." Then he morphed into the silhouette of a lamp.

In bed, sleep overtook Etta briefly, but only long enough to see the little girl standing there, undergarments held at her side, saying, "He is sorry. He was then, too." It brought her to full wakefulness. She arose in turmoil. Some strange vitality had seized her as surely as a cold winter wind. She could feel the mystery of her existence pressing in around her. Etta teetered at the edge of the steps before descending slowly to the kitchen. She poured herself a glass of milk and stared out the window into the dripping darkness.

"No ghosts," she said, gazing until the darkness itself began to change and she understood it was about to transform into something else, something made of light.

A trembling haze enveloped the kitchen, yet Etta didn't feel dizzy. Everything emanated waves of energy like heat, even the space between things. She felt it was all about to burst, to reveal the world as it was supposed to be. She readied herself for the chance to begin a new life, God willing. The room began to spread out around her, the floor fell out from below her, the ceiling receded into the heights, and Etta was floating free, her moment come at last.

ROBIN MARTZ CAME over in the morning for the cookies. Etta sometimes missed her knock, so she let herself in with the key under the spider plant and called out to her. Thinking she must be on the back porch, she walked on through the dining room, past the antique hutch that she loved so much, past the family picture with the dead boy and his dead father.

The first thing she saw as she approached the kitchen was the Tupperware container on the table filled; bless that woman's heart. Then, she turned to what seemed to be a pile of rags in the corner. Etta.

She rushed over to check for a pulse, but Etta was cold and beginning to stiffen. A wide smile remained on Etta's face and her eyes were open with expectation. Robin reached out and gently shut Etta's eyelids. They began to slowly open when she removed her hand and she held them closed again until they stayed. Robin cried, partly for the loss of her only real friend, partly because she never really knew the woman, and partly because she knew that there was no one else to weep. After a few minutes, she called 911.

When she hung up, she turned to see the cookies sitting there. It felt wrong to take them now, a violation somehow. Then again, the last thing the woman had done was a favor for her. It also felt wrong to let that gesture go for nothing.

The paramedic said it was probably a stroke. Robin couldn't watch when they moved Etta's body onto the gurney. She looked away and out the window at the birdfeeder. Despite being nearly empty of seed, several species of small birds crowded the perch, and occasionally, a millet hull would pop up into the air and fly over their heads. She remembered hearing that birds came to rely on feeders and could die if you stopped putting out food. Maybe Etta had told her that. She wondered if she should start feeding them, if that could be one way of remembering her friend.

When the paramedics had finished, she signed the form and told them she knew of no living relatives. The cute one put his hand on her shoulder, told her he was sorry, and gave her a sympathetic wink. She insisted they take the cookies.

Robin was reluctant to leave the house, even after they were gone. It was as if to leave, to close that door one last time, would shut the door on the woman's entire existence. She decided to take a last look around, periodically touching items, her mouth drawing tight and wide, squeezing a few more silent tears as she contemplated lonely oblivion. She stopped in front of the picture of Etta, her husband, and the little boy. It was the only photograph of them together that she'd ever seen, and she'd never found out what happened to them.

Back in the kitchen, she saw a cardinal at the feeder. It reminded her of the small porcelain cardinal figurine that sat in the baking cabinet. Barely an inch high, Robin recalled the day that Etta had pulled it from a box of teabags, so surprised and pleased. "It's the West Virginia state bird, you know," she had said. Now, Robin walked over, opened the glass door at the top of the cabinet, and took the figurine, putting it in her pocket. It would go in her kitchen window to remind her.

She walked back to Etta's kitchen window to see if she could get a better look at the cardinal eating from the feeder. As she leaned over the sink, he suddenly cocked his head and turned his eye toward her. Robin took a step backward, turning away, startled.

THE BIRD, ALSO startled, flew to the branches of a Catawba tree filled with small, white blooms in Etta's back yard. Summer was coming on and the sun had long since dried up the rain from the night before, leaving a fresh, green scent that pulled the plants from the ground and prompted the cardinal to puff out his chest, ruffle his feathers, and sing. He was a striking bird, bright red, every feather of his wings tipped in black. His tufted crown rose in a gracefully curved triangle, and his symmetrical mask, the blackest black, gave him the air of royalty.

The cardinal was the father of four generations of offspring. For his entire adult life, this place had been his domain. Some months back, in the last throes of winter, his mate had died.

And now something else had changed. Something was missing beyond the seed, some vital energy. He knew there would be no more food in the same way that animals flee long before the tsunami, and the forest falls silent before the earth erupts. His time here was finished.

The cardinal flew from the Catawba into the face of an oncoming gust of wind, a straggler from the night before that lifted him up above the house where he could see a woman walking up the road. He flew out over the treetops that marked his territory and, bolstered by sudden buoyancy, let himself be lifted even higher, until the knobby green mountains lay spread out before him.

The bird flattened his crown and climbed, a tiny red speck in the blue, intruding upon the realm of hawks and buzzards, and pushing farther upward. The cardinal did not ask himself why he did this. For all his three years, he only ever did what the moment required of him, acting on deep instinct and awareness. His small lungs, not made for these heights, struggled to take in oxygen as he penetrated a cloud.

Beating his wings with all his strength, the cardinal punched through the cloud and back into blue sky, climbing, ever climbing until, in a sudden explosion of brilliant red, gold, and white light, he discovered he was not a cardinal at all.

Inky-do

PULL IN CLOSER to the fire, boys. Aya, grab yourself another brew there…drink 'em if ya got 'em, heh-heh! Drink, and be merry, fellers. There ya go.

You got yourself sitchiated there, Dewey? Ned? Aya, smoke 'em if ya got 'em, too. Ol' Henry Harper don't judge the wacky tobaccy. You know that.

Looks like you got your tent all set up. This here's a good field for camping out, that's for sure. Maybe if you're lucky, you'll catch a gander of Old Stinky Joe tonight. Right down there by them woods, that's where I first saw him, peeking out at me.

I see y'all grinning.

Aya, I know you like the Old Stinky Joe stories, so I'll tell you a little about him that I probably told ya before. First thing to remember about Old Stinky Joe, of course, is the stinky part. One stout whiffa that good ol' boy can drop a person into a coma for fifteen years! Aya, don't laugh. That's the truth, ya know. Fifteen years. That there's the smell of the old wild, and us civilized folk can't hardly bear that no more.

I was a lucky one. Old Stinky Joe, he didn't just show up at my door all of a sudden-like; he watched me from the woods for a long time before he ever came close. That gave me a chance to absorb that nasty smell from a distance for a while. But don't you be fooled. It ain't easy. You can smell that old boy from a mile away. That's how ya know to look for him.

Now, it ain't entirely Joe's fault that he's so darn stinky. He *is* a three-thousand-year-old Bigfoot after all, and he ain't never had no proper bath 'cept a rainstorm or a dip in the river. Joe says only one person was ever able to put up with his stink on the first meeting, and that was Teddy Roosevelt.

Aya, that's right. Teddy Roosevelt. Teddy was out hunting moose with some friends when he got a whiff of Joe from two miles away and started tracking him with his nose. As they got closer and closer, Teddy's friends started a-droppin' one by one from the smell, ya know. But Teddy, he was a tough one, that feller, a Rough Rider, and he weren't gonna be stopped. He pressed on alone, and when he found Joe, he ran up to him and buried his nose right in Joe's hairy belly! Joe said he didn't rightly know what to do. Teddy took a big ol' whiff and started a-laughin' to beat the band. Then, he gave Joe a slap on the back and run off and created the national parks, Yellerstone, and such. True story there, boys. I ain't never told ya that one.

Yeah, ol' Joe's been around a while and seen many a sight. Told me many a story over a cup of tea on the back porch.

And tonight, I think I'll tell ya about Old Stinky Joe's third cousin fifteen times removed, a Bigfoot that lived forty-thousand years ago, by the name of Inky-do. Aya, Inky-do. Sounds funny, I know, but I have to tell ya, right from the beginning, that Inky-do, as a name, weren't real funny. Fact was, it was quite the insult to Joe's cousin, the last insult, ya might say. But seein' as how history is written by the victorious, we'll just stick with Inky-do tonight.

But I'll tell ya, the reason why Inky-do was such an insult were the fact that the gods give him that name, naming him after one of their own, and the Bigfoots, well, they never liked the gods all that much.

And ya can't really blame em, ya know. The gods were unsavory sorts, just a buncha horny space goats, lookin' for hot monkey love.

Aya, I hear ya laughin, but that there's the trutha things. Back in the day, there musta been a big ol' neon sign on the moon with a big arrow pointing to Earth that said, Hot Monkey Love! Get Yer Furry Fornicatin' Here! And those old perverts, they just couldn't resist.

The Bigfoots, as ya might understand, was a bit put out by these hairless space monkeys, come down from the sky in their burning silver birds, givin' the high, hard one to all those poor monkey girls that the Bigfoots considered their little cousins. Of course, the wretched babies was born soon after and they didn't have near enough hair to survive the glaciers and such, so the Bigfoots went to the gods and said, Hey fellers, these here critters got no place in this world. They ain't gonna survive. Maybe y'all oughtta think about using some rubbers or something.

Well, this one old god, Aynew, got in his dead bird and rose up in the sky and his old bird just started shining real bright-like and he said, I am the sun, you ignoramuses! And the Bigfoots, they started a-laughin' at him and said, Well, no, you ain't.

And well, boys, that started a tussle, and that there fracas went on for thousands of years. A Bigfoot can tear you in half if he's got half a mind to, but he don't have much of a chance against space-god laser-beam death-rays, no sir. So that there tussle didn't work out so well for the Bigfoots and that's how them fellers got to be so good at hiding.

For thousands of years, they hid in the hills and hollers, just trying to stay outta sight, until, one day, young Inky-do peeked out of the woods and saw the city of Er.

NOW, ER WAS the name of the city 'cause the people living there couldna hardly make up their minds about anything. Er, maybe we should do this. Er, maybe we should do that. Their king, a feller named Gilgiemesh, was the worst of 'em. Couldna hardly make up his mind bout nothin' 'tall. Maybe that was cuz he was one-part monkey and two-parts god.

See boys, much as ya might spec, the monkey humpin' never really stopped. Them gods, they was hooked on the monkey love, especially once the hairless offspring started looking more like them. Then, they got all high and mighty, thinkin' they was great creators and such, saying, Oh, look at us, our shinola really don't stink. What bright little monkey children we have! They started teaching the hairless monkeys to call themselves mankind and to take what they needed from the world around 'em.

And take they did, boys, more even than the gods wanted em to, heh-heh.

Now, Gilgiemesh hisself was eight-foot-tall, which was from the god side of him. But it was easy to see that a lot of him came from the god side. Why, nary a farmer's daughter escaped that boy's clutches, and he was always bored. He'd mosey up and down the streets of Er and here's how it'd go: some poor peasant would bow to him and Gilgiemesh would say, What'd you say, boy? And the feller would say he said nothin', and Gilgiemesh'd say, You called me a dog! And the feller would say, No, Lord. Sorry Lord, and other such things. Then, Gilgiemesh'd beat the tar out of him.

So, as you might spec, a lotta folks just pondered things indoors while the king was out looking fer trouble.

I see ya grinning again there, boys. You know somebody like that, eh?

Aya, one in ever town, I'd say.

So, it was one of them there days, when everyone was a-hidin', and Gilgiemesh was bored, and he walked up and down the walls of Er. He was awful proud of them walls. He's up there, looking at the woods out yonder and he sees Inky-do, peekin' out from behind a tree. Gilgiemesh fell clean off the wall, he was so surprised, and by the time he got back up there, Inky-do was gone.

Gilgiemesh hadn't never seen no Bigfoot before and asked the gods to tell him what was goin on here. Now, as ya might guess, that was a bit awkward for the gods, who was just embarrassed that there was still Bigfoots out there that they'd missed with their space-god laser-beam death-rays. They told Gilgiemesh it was just best to let 'em be.

But the young king said, Look fellers, I just caint get a decent fight no more. Now y'all better tell me what's a'goin on here, or I'm gonna go find that big ol' hairy gent myself.

The gods weren't none too crazy 'bout that idear neither. They figgered there was about a hundred Bigfoots in there, waitin' to tear their boy limb from limb.

So, they told Gilgiemesh they'd bring Inky-do to him and came up with a plan, kinda typical if'n ya ask me. They decided to call up one of their good-time girls, an especially horny goddess by the name of Shamhat.

You want me to do what? To a what? she said.

Don't laugh. Fornicatin' with a Bigfoot is no laughing matter, as you might imagine.

But that Shamhat was a trooper and she was all kinda hot to trot too, so she headed out there and started parading around all nekkid and such, a-moanin' about how she wished she had herself a big, ol' hairy boy to do what her husband couldn't. And, well, sooner or later, Inky-do, being a young buck after all, and prone to a bad decision or two—ya know how that goes, boys—said what the hey and went for it. He banged that old girl for a week straight and, by the time it was over, she'd clean passed out, so Inky-do took her back to Er, slung over his shoulder, all limp and wrung out.

And Gilgiemesh was waiting for him at the gate.

IT WAS A fight, boys, lemme tell ya. Them two wrestled for seven days themselves, and truthfully, if Inky-do hadn't a-been shaggin' for a week previous, it woulda been over quicker, but eventually, Gilgiemesh wore out and Inky-do pinned him down and asked him if he'd had enough.

You're one tough old boy, said Gilgiemesh. Ain't no one ever whupped me like that before.

Well, I was tired, said Inky-do, and they both laughed and started clappin' each other on the back, and by this time Shamhat had woke up and said, I don't know what y'all are laughin' about, and went walkin' home all bowlegged.

As you might spec, the people of Er was all happy about how things had turned out. Now there was somebody to take the heat offa them, so they all came back outside, just plum amazed to meet Inky-do when Gilgiemesh started touring him round the town.

He took Inky-do to the sandal maker and said, look at these here fine sandals, and Inky-do said a Bigfoot don't need no sandals, besides, they don't have my size. And he took him to the jewelery maker and said, Look at these fine jewels, and Inky-do said, Can I eat them? And he took him to the glass maker, and Inky-do said, Why not just drink from the crick?

And he took him to the farm, and Inky-do said, Did those plants want to grow there? Or did you force 'em to? And he took him to a monument built to the gods, and Inky-do asked, Will it last as long as the mountain?

Gilgiemesh was just plain flummoxed by all of this and said, Look at them there walls I built. Now, you ain't gonna tell me that those ain't awesome!

They's impressive, said Inky-do, but I'm not really sure what they's good fer.

Well, they keep out the tigers and such, said Gilgiemesh.

What would ya wanna keep out the tigers for? asked Inky-do.

Tigers kill the babies, said Gilgiemesh, and Inky-do laughed.

Of course, they do, he said. That's what they's made fer. I'd get used to it if I were you.

And now Gilgiemesh was all put out and got quiet.

Inky-do said, I can see why yer bored, Gilgiemesh. There just ain't nothin real about any of this here stuff. You should come with me and see the world you really live in.

Gilgiemesh was plain outta idears, so he said okay, and they headed out into the hills and hollers.

ALONG THE WAY, Inky-do told him about how the Bigfoots considered the land and life around them to be their relatives and showed Gilgiemesh all the small wonders of the world, the ways the insects and the plants and the birds and the animals worked together in their savage paradise. Them woods was much like these woods round here in West Virginny, boys, and Inky-do showed him the watery world of the fishes, the high and haughty hawks, the far-fetched flight of the geese, the tireless dig of the groundhog, the amazing teamwork of the tiny ants and bees. He showed him how the water and wind carved stone and earth, how the trees captured the sun, and how the earth called the lightning from the skies, and Gilgiemesh was plum amazed at it all.

Gilgiemesh said, But these are all created by the gods, yes?

Inky-do just laughed and said that all these things had been there long before the gods came.

But that ain't how they told us it was at all, said the young king. They told me y'all was ogres and the world was just filled with ways to die.

And so it is, said Inky-do, and ain't it just a beautiful thing?

Now, Inky-do was a young Bigfoot and missed all them tussles with the gods, but he told Gilgiemesh what he knew about all that and promised to take him to visit his uncle, an old Bigfoot named Humbubba, who lived off to the west in the forest and knew all about them times.

That night, Inky-do and Gilgiemesh slept under the stars, and Gilgiemesh had hisself a strange dream where he was nekkid with a big old stiffy standing in front of the people of Er and not a farmer's daughter in sight.

NOW, BOYS, THE gods knew all about Inky-do's uncle. Humbubba lived in the great cedar forest and the gods, well, they was itchin' pretty bad to get in there and cut down some of them trees so their women could have nice cedar chests for their quilts and such. But ever time one of 'em went in there to try and chop one down, he'd come home all blue

and purple with bruises and a story about how rocks came
from everwhere and nowheres.

But the gods couldn't never find Humbubba, and they
was sore angry about that.

So Inky-do and Gilgiemesh didn't realize that the gods
had followed them right on down to that old cedar forest
and was a-waitin' and watchin' when old Humbubba came
out to see his nephew.

At first, Humbubba wouldn't come out. Whatchoo
doin', Inky-do? he hollered. That's one of them there gods
you brought into my woods. Don't you know no better'n
that?

This one here's different, Inky-do hollered back.

Then, Gilgiemesh stepped forward, dodging the rocks,
and began speaking in a voice like a strong lovely song, so
sincere that sparrows flew down and landed on his shoulders.
He said that he hadn't never really seen the fishes before, or
the hawks, or the ants, or the groundhogs, or the geese. He
said he was sorry about what his folks had done, and that he
wanted to understand why they was all feudin' so as he could
help everybody be friends again, and afore too long,
Humbubba decided that this feller might be alright after all,
and he come out from behind the trees.

So Gilgiemesh, Inky-do, and Humbubba went and sat
down under a hundred-foot tall cedar tree and Humbubba
started tellin' Gilgie 'bout the beginning of days. But no
sooner did he start than the tree split down the middle with
a great crack and burst into flames. As they ran away from the
falling timber, a humongous, fiery beast of metal and smoke
rose from behind the hill. It kinda looked like a bull with two
straight horns and then, outta them horns, come two space-

god laser-beam death-rays, and ol' Humbubba's head rolled clean off his body, all a-smokin' like.

Well, boys, a scream of rage from a Bigfoot is a thing a mortal man don't never wanna hear, and Inky-do let one out that blew the windows outta that spaceship. Humbubba was his favorite uncle and the only one of his kin that lived nearby. Inky-do was so mad that he ran over and took aholda half of that burning tree and started spinning it round his head so that Gilgiemesh had to hit the dirt to keep from gettin' knocked into next week. Then, Inky-do let it fly and it speared that old mechanical bull right through the belly and the beast came crashing down, burnin' and 'splodin' all over the place.

Inky-do was having a right serious conniption fit. He turned back around to Gilgiemesh and said, I thought you was my friend! And Gilgiemesh said, I am your friend! I didn't know them yahoos was comin'!

But Inky-do was tearin' at his own fur and told Gilgiemesh he could go blow. Then he took off into the forest. Gilgiemesh couldn't hardly keep up, and afore you know it, Inky-do was gone.

AS YOU MIGHT imagine, the gods was hoppin' mad about losing their flying livestock, but Gilgiemesh wasn't none too happy neither. He went back home to Er and demanded that someone do some explaining.

One of the gods by the name of Enlittle came out and stood afront of Gilgiemesh like a mad schoolteacher.

Why'd y'all kill my friend's uncle? asked Gilgie.

'Cause he was a monster who was hurtin' your kin, said Enlittle.

He wadn't a-hurtin' nobody, said Gilgiemesh. He was just hidin' behind trees and throwin' rocks.

Well, you should see some of the bruises he left, said Enlittle. Some of 'em didn't go away for weeks.

Listen now, I'm serious, said Gilgiemesh. That ol' boy Inky-do was my friend and now he thinks I'm a real snake in the grass. Why'd you do it?

To create jobs, said Enlittle. People need jobs.

Gilgiemesh started a-spittin' and fumin' and said, Do *what*?!

Enlittle looked at his fingernails and said, Gilgiemesh, you are a king. You has to create jobs for all these folk you been beating up. Now, that old monster Humbubba, he was just a-gettin' in the way of progress, out there, throwin' all those hard, sharp rocks. Now, is you the king? Or what?

Gilgiemesh didn't rightly know what to say to this. He *was* the king, so maybe Enlittle had a point there. But still, there was that matter of the fishes and the ants and the groundhogs and the hawks.

That there feller was lying to ya about all that, said Enlittle. The gods created all that stuff, so, since we made it, we's allowed to destroy it. You better be careful or we'll destroy you, too!

So why'd you create ol' Humbubba, then? asked Gilgiemesh.

You just mind yer tongue, said Enlittle.

NOW, GILGIEMESH WAS more tore up than ever. Something just didn't seem right about all of this, but he just could not decide what to do. He walked around all hangdog, and insteada runnin' off and hidin' like they used to, the folk in Er started to pity him just a little. And when the gods saw this, they thought maybe they should do something about it before them folks started asking awkward questions. Because, as much as the gods looked at people like their monkey-love slaves, humans was actually turning out to be a bit smarter than they figgered. It was gettin' harder and harder to keep some stuff from 'em. And sure as shootin', they didn't want their hairless monkeys knowing all their secrets. For that matter, they didn't want 'em understanding the hawks, or the groundhogs, or the ants, or the fishes, neither. They was thinking they might have to do something drastic in the future.

But something had to be done about the young king now.

What do we do? asked one of the gods.

And another said, Maybe we should get him a little nookie.

But he done had all the farmer's daughters, said the first. Who's left?

The second said, How about Ishtar? She's a sport.

The first wrinkled his face up like a pug dog and said, Better him than me. Don't she have some social disease?

A bunch. said the second. See? It all works out.

Ishtar was a goddess and she was more than willing to help, 'cause she thought Gilgiemesh was one fine hairless monkey.

They got her all dolled up in her sexiest pink nighty and…

…I see you boys got a picture in your head there…

Aya, don't laugh now, cause any good ol' boys that got to fornicatin' with Ishtar weren't likely to be around for long. She was what they call the fem fay-tall.

She came a-slinkin' out of the sunset one evening, putting the mojo on ol' Gilgiemesh, and reaching under his sheepskin kilt. But as it was, Gilgie just couldn't get it up for her. The truth was that he really did love his friend, Inky-do, and he just didn't have no drive no more. It seemed like the world was one way, but he was told it was another by the only folk he ever trusted. It was confusing, and how could he ever get in the mood for lovin' when his friend thought he was a rat bastard? He pushed Ishtar's hand out from under his kilt, which was probably better for him all around anyway, and he went to find his walking pack.

Something just wasn't right about all this, and somewheres in the back of his mind he made his choice. He was choosing the ants, and the geese, and the fishes, and the trees. He was gonna find his hairy friend, Inky-do.

Boys, maybe you seen a woman scorned before. I'd wager you seen at least one. A goddess scorned is about three hundred and sixty-five thousand times worse.

As soon as Gilgiemesh took to hoofin', Ishtar started raisin a ruckus to Enlittle and the rest. Said she wanted Gilgiemesh or Inky-do dead, and she'd be happy with either one.

NOW, GILGIEMESH ROAMED the mountains and valleys, looking for his friend, and while Inky-do watched him from hidden places, the young king called out his apologies to all the living things he'd disrespected. He stopped at the streams and spoke with the fish. He hollered into the hills, tellin' the groundhogs that he was sorry for callin' 'em big rats. He bowed to the hawks and the ancient trees and asked them if they'd seen his good friend Inky-do. For seven days and seven nights, Gilgiemesh pushed on, before the burning silver birds of the gods came a-swoopin' out of the sky, chasing him across the fields with their space-god laser-beam death-rays, burning the ground around his feet.

Now, Inky-do knew that his friend was true, and he let out a scream to curl your toes. He jumped out from his hiding place on the hillside and grabbed two stones, each the size of a man's head. He took those stones and threw 'em at the ships like Dizzy Dean fastballs and knocked one of them silver birds clean outta the sky.

Gilgiemesh saw him and let out a war whoop of his own, grabbing more stones and lettin' 'em fly. Next thing ya know, them ships are droppin' like dead bugs. Inky-do roared and Gilgiemesh roared and the power of their friendship plucked the gods from the sky and cast them to Earth in smoky ruin, and, as the last one spun to Earth, it cast its red beams of death in all directions like drownin' hands looking for purchase.

WELL BOYS, NOW I gotta warn ya that this here is where the story gets a little weepy-like, cause Gilgiemesh looked over at the hillside to see Inky-do, lookin' down at a smoking hole in his chest the size of a Campbell's soup can. He ran 'cross the field as fast as he could but couldn't get there before his friend fell over dead.

Now, it's hard fellers, when you're holdin' on to a friend that's gone, you take my word for it, 'cause I know, I done it.

You sit there and you look at 'em and the sadness is purt near comin' outta every part of ya, and it don't take long afore you look away for someone else's eyes, someone who can see how bad you're hurtin', someone who can understand, and there ain't nothin' more plum awful than when they ain't nobody there, 'cause you want the world to take note. At times like that, boys, you want the whole damn world to just stop, just stop. And the world, well, it never does, no sir. No, sir…

Now Gilgiemesh, he held Inky-do's head in his lap, and after a few minutes, he let out a moan that shook the ground for seven miles around. He carried his friend to the top of the mountain where he built a pyre overlooking the valley and set it a-burnin'. Then, he stood on the edge of the cliff there and, while Inky-do's body burned, he yelled out into the air.

This was my friend, Inky-do! he hollered. He was a fine feller and a proud Bigfoot and I am honored to have known him! He was the best friend I ever had, who taught me about the fishes, and the ants, and the hawks, and the groundhogs, and the geese, and the trees, and the wind, and the rain, and the lightning, and on and on he went for days on end, long after the fire had gone out and only pieces of bones remained.

Gilgiemesh never thought no one heard him.

But there was a small tribe of folk though, who had just kinda wandered off from the gods a long while back, living on their own in the hills and hollers. They heard the sad song of Gilgiemesh, and it made them wonder.

NOW, GILGIEMESH FELT he had to atone, like we all do when we lose someone and feel that we're to blame. He ripped the clothes from his body and ran nekkid into the wild where he wandered, half-crazy, calling out to the other Bigfoots, fighting lions with his bare hands, talking to dead people and invisible sailors.

Of course, the Bigfoots knew he was out there, but there weren't none of 'em to want to talk to him. For twenty years, he wandered the woods, and then one day, he used the last of his mad strength.

He fell over dead, right then and there, and Gilgiemesh, the king, was no more.

AND THAT'S THE truth of it, boys, though I'd not go so far as to say it's carved in stone. That's the way Ol' Stinky Joe told me, one night over a pot of pekoe in the moonlight.

But, wait now! The story ain't quite over yet!

You see, Shamhat—you remember that ol' girl? Well, turns out, after she recuperated herself from her week in the woods with Inky-do, she discovered she was in the family way. Now, nothin' coulda been more embarrassing to Enlittle, Ishtar, and the others, so they hid her away until she had the child, and they cast the infant into the wilderness when he was born. That child was found by the hill people who took him in and named him Cain. Cain fathered many children in his day and that, my young friends, was how Bigfoot blood passed into human beings.

You can always tell those of us that got it, boys. You can always tell.

So, there ya go. That'll do it for ol' Henry tonight, I think. I'm too pooped to pop and it looks to be you fellers got a lot more beer drinkin' to do. So, if you would do me a favor and make sure that there fire is out before y'all cash in for the night, I surely would appreciate it.

And keep your nose to the breeze boys. Keep your nose to the breeze.

The Eighth Angel

DOGLEG BEND. HIS third and final stop in West Virginia. Roy Cross got out of his car on Main Street and glanced around. The town appeared dead already. Sometimes, he wondered what good he could do in places like this, but he was not to question the will of the Lord. Hills rose on three sides of the dilapidated downtown, all two blocks of it. On the western side, it sloped toward a river, reminding him of the opening to a cave. Maybe it was just the low-hanging clouds that made the place so dreary, he thought, looking up at the gray sky.

And that's when the toad hit him right in the eye.

SPLAT.

It was an obscene noise, like from a dirty movie, the sound of flesh slapping flesh, and, if he hadn't been so surprised, he might have taken a moment to register his disgust. But the soft body of the toad perfectly filled the hollow of his eye socket, giving the slap a lurid resonance that echoed across the quiet thoroughfare.

"Holy fuckin' shit!" came a voice from across the street. Cross looked through his watery vision to see two young men running toward him, at least one of whom was laughing, still saying, "Holy fuckin' shit! Did you see that?"

"It's a fuckin' toad, man! Look! The thing just dropped outta the sky, dude!"

"Holy shit! It's alive!"

"Kill it!"

"No way! Fuckin' thing just fell outta the sky and now it's hoppin' away like it's fuckin' Supertoad or somethin'."

"Would you please stop cursing?" Roy Cross was starting to come to his senses and resented the unnecessary vulgarity. The sound was still bouncing around in his brain and now he understood its familiarity, furthering his confusion and anger.

"You okay, man?" asked one.

"Fucking thing just fell out of the sky!"

"Yes, I'm okay. And please!"

"*Frickin'* thing just *frickin'* fell out of the *frickin'* sky!"

"The Lord sends signs," said Cross, still trying to clear the water from his eyes, "to warn us of the End of Days." His face was flushed with embarrassment and he wondered how many people saw it happen.

"Uh-huh," said one. "You're probably gonna have a shiner there."

"I'm fine! I'm fine. Thank you. You can go." Cross didn't like to attract this much attention when he got into a town.

The two stood there looking at him for a second. He still could not see them clearly.

"The Lord sent a fuckin' toad, dawg," said one, and they walked away, laughing. Just before they left earshot, he heard the other say, "You suppose he'll get a wart on his eyeball?"

The toad disappeared under a bush.

Cross got back in his car. He wondered if the job was compromised. Inordinate attention. But this was just a podunk little place and there hadn't been anyone around other than those two boys, even in the middle of town and the middle of a Saturday. His plan had been to do his business at the diner today and the Dogleg Bend Baptist Church tomorrow. With slowly clearing sight, he scanned the surroundings from his car. No one else in sight. No one looking.

He examined his eye in the tilted rearview mirror. Yes, it was going to swell, but all in all, it didn't hurt as badly as the fish in New Haven.

The diner appeared to be useless for his plans at the moment. He could see only a few figures through the front window. He would wait until it was a little busier, but looking around, he wondered if that would ever happen. He sat in his car until his vision began to feel normal again, donned a pair of sunglasses, and got out to take in the town.

AS HE WALKED, he was periodically reminded of his old life. There was an old hardware store, closed at noon according to the sign, with wooden shelves lining its walls filled with dusty merchandise. He remembered one just like it in Dellroy, Ohio, and he thought of the times he and Mary Ann had spent there, asking Leonard what they needed in the ongoing effort to fix up their old house. Those were the good years, filled with the blessings of God.

For it truly was God, and his angel Mary Ann, who had rescued Roy from the demon alcohol, and he had clutched onto both with a fervent devotion. First, Mary Ann's eyes with their blue-gray compassion and the way they became the ocean when she loved, when she called him from his exile, the eyes of his mother opening the door to the closet. Her eyes struck a chord deep within him and he remembered, then, the times that God had spoken to him in the hot thirsty black of the wardrobe.

So, it was that God spoke to him again in the drunken darkness and asked him, *"My child, how could you forget? Who was there for you but Me?"* Mary Ann's eyes and his newfound memories of the voice of the Lord gave him the determination to crawl from the pit of his life, and he dedicated himself to both with an energy that consumed his days. His holy obsessions.

They attended church functions three days a week and twice on Sundays. Willard, from the church, had helped him land a job as a custodian at a nearby university, and Cross dedicated his free hours to understanding the teachings of the God who had freed him. In the evening, he and Mary Ann watched televangelists, including the Reverend Jack Van Impe.

Early on, he found himself fascinated by Van Impe and the subject of biblical prophecy. He occupied much of his time divining the essence of Daniel's visions, of Ezekiel, and the Revelation of Saint John, and it was clear the end could not be far away. He would lie in bed and talk about it with Mary Ann. They would thank the Lord that they were saved and talk about how awful it would be if they weren't. Cross began to understand the wickedness of the world.

Eventually, knowing that the word must be spread, that mankind had to be warned, he started his own website, *endtimesacomin.com*. There, he would post links to news stories that showed the prophecies coming true: pestilences, earthquakes, debauchery, famine.

At times, Mary Ann would tire of it.

"Can't we just forget it all? For just one night?"

In those moments, he would hug her. A woman needs attention; he knew this.

"I can't wait until the day comes when we walk in eternal love, away from the pain of this world," Roy said, squeezing her tightly.

"Is there no light here?" Her hug was loose, her body limp with surrender.

One night, Mary Ann sat with him as he posted links to articles about a new strain of flu rampaging through Asia. Above the website links, he put a picture of an Asian woman in a surgical mask, tears streaming from her bloodshot eyes, a baby in her arms and a headline below the picture, which read, "Death Toll Nears 1,000."

As he considered his design, he became aware that Mary Ann's breathing seemed uneven. He turned to see her eyes glued to the screen, tears rolling over her cheekbones.

"I know," he said. "It's sad. God have mercy on us."

"It's not just that," she said. The tears streamed even harder.

"What? What is it, sweetheart?"

"The innocents…"

"But the innocents are taken straight into God's loving embrace, honey. You know that."

She turned to look at him, a horrified expression on her face.

"What am I hoping for?" she asked, but Cross wasn't sure she was talking to him and didn't know what to say. She rose, still crying, and left the room.

Later, when he crawled into bed beside her, her back was turned to him and he tried not to disturb her. As he closed his eyes, he heard her say, "Maybe we should have a baby, Roy."

"I don't know," said Cross. "Do you think it's a good thing to bring a child into a world like this?"

She never answered.

SOMETHING CHANGED IN Mary Ann that night. From then on, she seemed less enthusiastic about the website. The bedtime talks about the blessings of the Lord, the Rapture, and the End Days were less frequent, and she participated less actively, mostly just agreeing with his observations. The behavior struck him as curiously familiar, and that was when he first perceived it at church.

One Wednesday evening, after his adult Bible study class let out early, Cross went to the church bathroom to relieve himself while waiting for Mary Ann to finish choir practice. As he washed his hands, he thought about the point he'd been arguing about the seven angels a few moments earlier. What a shame that Terry Philips broke up the group prematurely. Some people just couldn't accept the truth when it was right in front of them.

Drying his hands, he could hear the choir outside the door, coming out of the sanctuary. He reached for the knob and, as the door cracked, he heard Jim Penney say, "Where's Mr. End-of-the-World?" A couple of the women tittered and Mary Ann replied, "He's probably waiting outside." There was no light in her voice. Cross slid the door shut. As he waited for them to pass, he could smell mothballs and felt imaginary clothes, hanging over him, brushing the top of his hair.

It bothered him, the sniping tone of Jim's comment and Mary Ann's weary reply, but he said nothing.

By now, *endtimesacomin.com* was getting twenty to thirty visitors a day. He received an email from a Ronald Smalls of Barnwell, South Carolina, saying, "Bless you folks. Your website is one of the best I've ever seen. I check it every day. You are doing the work of the Lord and I thank you."

The implication that he, Roy Cross, was having an *effect*, that he was playing a part in the unfolding of the Lord's Plan, was new to him. It felt wondrous, magical, and it made Jim Penney seem small and insignificant.

He related his success to his wife every evening.

"That's great, Roy," she'd say. "God must be proud of you."

The website was just beginning to take off when Mary Ann left him.

At first, he was bewildered. It didn't make sense, this "life with you was too dark" stuff. In Roy's mind, they were fighting the darkness together, resisting the tide of evil, preparing to usher in a new age with the arrival of Lord Jesus. He had only ever envisioned that moment with her by his side. He figured it was just a mistake that she would soon recognize. When she didn't come back, he knew deep in his heart that they would be reunited in time for the Resurrection. He had faith, even while signing the divorce papers in her lawyer's office.

"In the eyes of God, you're still my wife," he said, handing her the pen.

When he heard that she'd married Jim Penney, he confronted her on the street outside the library.

"He sings," Mary Ann said. She touched his arm, her look full of pity.

As she walked away, he yelled, "You're still my wife!" but she didn't turn around.

Cross did not understand why God was punishing him, taking his wife and even his church, where it was clear he was no longer wanted. He cried into his pillow every morning when he went to bed, worn out from mopping university floors all night with the ferocity of a cornered beast.

BUT THAT WAS all a long time ago, and Cross was alone now, strengthened by the Lord's work. He was bored with this dead little hamlet and, for now, he'd managed to mostly push the toad from his mind. Small crowd or no, he was going to complete the diner part of the job.

He went back to his car, pulled the Styrofoam container from its bag, and opened the top, removing a test-tube with a hinged cap from a form-fitted slot. After this, only one tube remained. He stuck the test tube in his trouser pocket and headed for the diner.

AFTER DISCOVERING THAT Mary Ann had gone the way of the harlot, Cross worked doubly hard on the website and put in more hours at work, trying to avoid idle time and the temptations of the internet. He read the Holy Bible daily and tried to understand his purpose. Surely he'd been saved for a reason. Was it love or vengeance? It began to consume him. Purpose. Destiny. There would come a day when Mary Ann would see his true fate, and she would cry that she hadn't stayed by his side. It would be part of her eternal torment and he would cry to see her suffer, but God demanded justice. Cross demanded it, too.

He became more and more intrigued by the refrigerators in the laboratory at the university. "Biological Hazard," the signs warned. "Authorized Personnel Only." Their red and yellow messages pulled at his attention every night.

"We never mop in there," his boss said to him once. "That room is always locked because that's where they keep the germs."

The germs. It fascinated Cross that pandemic lurked behind that glass. It fascinated him that the warning signs bore a sigil of three crescent moons atop a circle, a sun. It fascinated him enough to try the door handle every night until the night he found it unlocked, surely the work of the Lord.

THREE CITIES IN each state, for the Father, the Son, and the Holy Ghost. Cross chose the cities by pinning a road map to the wall, closing his eyes and throwing darts. The Lord guided his hand as he shuffled the state maps and drew one at random. The Lord guided the darts.

Cross had stolen six dozen test-tubes from the refrigerator that night, all packed in Styrofoam containers. He put them gingerly into a trash bag and left the room quickly, locking the door behind him. He carried the bag out with the rest of the trash and didn't stop, taking them to his car and driving straight home, not even clocking out. At home, he packed the containers into coolers with ice and loaded them into the back of his car.

He took nothing from the house except for his clothes and the wooden carving of crucified Jesus that hung over the bed he used to share with Mary Ann. He pictured her moaning and thrusting under Jim Penney, beneath a different cross, perhaps beneath a Satanic pentagram. He drove into town, withdrew his savings, and left Dellroy forever. Cross drove north to Geneva, where he paid cash to rent a cottage on the lake. With his holy treasure stowed in the refrigerator, he slept on the bare floor under the crucifix, listened to the Erie waves lapping in the night, and prayed for the Lord to reveal the full extent of His plan.

Cross preferred to target restaurants and malls. High-traffic was best, but retail locations could be tricky as one might be taken for a shoplifter, or worse, a terrorist. Churches were his favorite. *"For this light momentary affliction is preparing us for an eternal weight of glory beyond all comparison."*

Cross was the instrument of the affliction.

This was not terrorism. It was not about sending a message. This was secret work, a means to a larger end, and he was a part of it, making it happen. Roy Cross took on his solitary, holy work with the devotion it deserved. Over the next year, the Lord had guided him by map and dart, up and down the east coast of the United States, from Maine, to Florida, and now to Dogleg Bend, West Virginia. He had only ever been sick once. God protected him. He was the herald of the apocalypse, the bringer of Armageddon.

And now, he'd been hit in the eye by a toad.

After a piece of cherry pie, when no one was looking, Cross released the cap from the test-tube hidden in his palm, waved his arms up in a fake stretch, and proceeded to the rest room, touching everything near him. When the deed was done, he left Millie's Diner, letting his hand linger on the doorknob, sliding slowly from the brass as the door closed behind him.

CROSS EXAMINED HIS eye in the Motel 6 bathroom mirror. It was a light bluish-purple, not as bad as it could have been, he supposed. His mind again lit on the memory of seeing that formless lump with its amphibian feet spread to the sky just before it collided with his face. And again, disquiet struck him as he heard the salacious noise echo through his memory, awakening thoughts of New Haven afresh. He stood there, gently poking and pressing the swollen flesh around his eye. Was God throwing things at him? He'd heard of toads and fish falling from the sky; he had put such things on his website years before, but usually there was more than *one* fish or toad. He turned from his reflection and back to the bed, where he opened up his Bible to a passage in First Peter that he'd marked right after the fish.

"Beloved do not be surprised at the fiery trial when it comes upon you to test you, as though something strange were happening to you. But rejoice insofar as you share Christ's sufferings, that you may also rejoice and be glad when his glory is revealed."

It did not soothe him as quickly as when he'd first found it, so he read it over and over, until the image of flying amphibians left his mind.

Later, he purchased fried chicken from Walmart and ate it in his room. Then, he pulled his church clothes from his valise and used the hotel iron to press off his suit before he went to bed. He wanted to look his best for services.

The next morning, Roy Cross went to church.

THE WOODEN CHURCH was bigger and whiter than it needed to be for this town, but Cross was happy to see the pedestal fans in lieu of air conditioning. It would be a hot-closet, thirsty day. He would park himself right behind one of the fans.

The preacher caught him at the door to the chapel, a smug-looking fellow who introduced himself as Pastor Mooney and who seemed infinitely curious about his church's latest visitor. Cross fed him the usual story of being a traveling pharmaceutical salesman. Forgetting himself in the heat, he almost spoke of his father's devotion to his salvation. Instead, he gave the standard tale of his family's involvement with the church, denominationally flavored, of course.

Pastor Mooney bragged to him about the church being a hundred-twenty years old and founded by his great-great-grandfather, a "Baptist warrior" who had driven the witches from the hills. The man was so self-righteous and filled with pride that it reminded Cross of why churches were his favorite targets in the first place. His father would have known. There was no real worship anymore. They were all filled with hypocrites who would turn on you in a second. They were all filled with singing men who coveted other men's wives.

The pastor finally freed him when the deacon pointed at his watch. Cross entered the chapel, where he sat in the back corner, next to one of the fans. From here, no one could see what he was doing. Several paper fans were waving in the congregation of perhaps thirty-five parishioners.

Members turned to scrutinize him, mildly disapproving looks on their faces, as if Cross had purposely kept Pastor Mooney from getting on with it. The preacher's welcome from the pulpit prompted the rest of the congregation to turn and look at him. Cross smiled and nodded and, before long, they had forgotten him and the sermon had begun.

At one point, Mooney spoke of visiting an elderly woman, a former parishioner. Arthritis had twisted her up in pain and the minister spoke for ten minutes about the elegance of her faith, closing the story with a quote from Second Corinthians, "And he said unto me, My grace is sufficient for thee: for my strength is made perfect in weakness. Most gladly therefore will I rather glory in my infirmities, that the power of Christ may rest upon me."

"Amen," Cross said under his breath as he pulled the test-tube from his jacket pocket.

He imagined that the germs he loosed upon the world would one day break into a pandemic, whole cities and governments would fall, and Christ would descend from the clouds with his sword to find his faithful soldier, Roy Cross, waiting for his reward for spreading holy disease among the golden calf worshippers and unfaithful wives. In reality, he knew nothing about the germs he had stolen: common, low-level rhinoviruses, used for drug testing.

And Roy Cross, the eighth angel of the apocalypse, opened the vial upon the face of the Earth, and lo, there fell a noisome and grievous case of coughs, fevers, body aches, and runny noses.

Daddy had nothing on Roy Cross.

AS CROSS DROVE out of town, he crested a hill just south of Dogleg Bend, and the vista opened on a brown and gray landscape that stretched as far as he could see. On one side of the road, there were still trees and hills. On the other, all green just stopped, like it had reached the edge of the underworld.

The land to the south was leveled and scraped clean, terraced and dead, angled and ordered, a chunk of the world torn away. Clearly, nothing could rise here unless it was hideous. The emptiness of it hit his gut like the toad hit his eye, formless, shadowed, sudden, and obscene. He'd never seen anything like it. It was an abomination. Surely, he thought, my work is coming to an end.

As he drove past the barren landscape, he imagined that the Antichrist sat out on that desolate plain, smoke, death, and laughter coiling from his seven heads, blood dripping from his ten horns, ready to devour the world. He shuddered at the monsters loose on the Earth.

Restraint

HE TRIES NOT to think about her.

Flying out Corwin Road at sixty miles an hour, lights flashing and siren whooping, Deputy Sheriff Tommy Price pushes the afternoon's memories down into the bedrock of his subconscious and attempts to focus on Trudy Stevens. Trudy, the very pleasant woman who's waited on him at Millie's Diner every Tuesday and Thursday for the last seven years, has placed a call to 911. Domestic violence incident with injuries. Ambulance dispatched. Price speeds toward her address through the dark, the cruiser gliding smoothly over the potholed road, as if it has power over all of life's rough surfaces. The events of last week, of earlier that day even, rampage into his thoughts, fresh, raw, and all-encompassing, dwarfing all thoughts of duty or responsibility. He focuses on the road, keeping a wary eye out for deer in his high beams as the shadows of trees fly back into mountain darkness. The bucks are in rut and hunting season is approaching. They're always on the move, especially at night.

To his left, the trees clear, suddenly replaced by a barbed wire fence which separates the road from a field that slopes away, gently at first, illuminated at the top by the partial moonlight, plunging quickly into black. Around the next turn, he sees Deputy Pete Beck's flashing lights. Pete has arrived first, which tells Price that the younger deputy has been down the road visiting his girlfriend.

Despite the fact that other cars do occasionally patrol here, the Dogleg Bend area has more or less belonged to Price since he moved down this way seven years before. Residential real estate was cheaper with the strip mining so close, and he'd gotten a good deal on a house when the elderly owner passed away. His boss, Junior, had given him a bonus out of his own pocket to help with the purchase. When he tried to refuse it, Junior had said, "No, now Tommy-boy, you take it. I gotta lotta faith in you, son. Once you're all settled down there, I want you to represent me to those folks around Dogleg Bend, eh? Make sure they're still gonna vote for Junior Johnson, you savvy?"

Trudy's trailer is set back up on the hill to the left, an eroded gravel driveway descending to the road, where Price pulls in behind Pete's cruiser. A concrete garage stands off to the trailer's right, in front of which Pete is talking to Trudy, who waves her arms under the sharp garage floodlight as she speaks. In the driveway, a man who looks to be in his mid-sixties lies supine on his back, occasionally lifting his head and shouting at the sky, pounding his fists in the dirt. Price hears the drone of his voice through the closed cruiser window. The ambulance has not arrived yet.

Price sighs. At least Trudy seems okay. Good. She knows how he likes his coffee. He puts on his hat, grabs his notebook, and shuts off the cruiser. Pete is walking toward him, down the driveway.

Deputy Price had taken it seriously when Bergen County Sheriff Junior Johnson said he wanted him to represent the department in this town. He made it a point to join a local church, dined at Millie's twice a week, attended picnics and festivals, made courtesy calls, helped put up signs around election time, and generally tried to be a good person, friendly and helpful like a police officer should. He guessed that was why his neighbor, Kermit Hamrick, had come to him for help two weeks ago, and why he'd finally decided to do as the man requested.

He takes a deep breath and tries to concentrate on the job at hand.

"YOU'RE NOT GOING to believe this one, Tommy," says Pete.

"You get Trudy's statement?"

"Some of it. Tommy, you ain't gonna believe it. This fella over here—"

"Wallace Stevens, yeah, I know who he is." The man in the driveway mumbles to himself. Trudy has moved over to the wooden porch built onto the front of the trailer, under the yellow light.

Pete looks at his notebook. "Well, uh, he's run over."

"You killed me, woman!" Wallace yells, as if he knows he is being talked about.

"If I could only be so lucky." Trudy spits. "*Wally.*" This version of the woman is a new sight to Deputy Price.

"Wal—" the man lying in the driveway pounds the dirt. "Oh, I swear, woman! If I weren't crippled up!"

"He don't like being called Wally." Pete snickers.

"Alright, alright," Price says, "you go up there and finish interviewing Trudy, and I'll see what I can get out of Wally here before the ambulance comes."

"You really ain't gonna believe this one."

"Okay, okay."

Pete walks up to the porch with his pad and pencil and Deputy Price approaches Wallace, still groaning and mumbling. A single muddy tire track runs across his blue jeans at thigh level.

"Mr. Stevens?"

"I was," Wallace moans, looking at the sky as if he is seeing hosts of angels. "She done killed me with my own truck."

Price can't see any blood, but there's no denying the tire track.

"My *own* truck, man; it's just wrong."

"You want to tell me how all this happened?"

"Aw, officer," he says, grimacing. "You know, I was just trying to show my wife some love is all." He grumbles something about being thirty years faithful and the talk soon degenerates into the type of bullshit that any ten-year law enforcement officer learns to tune out. Tonight, though, he finds that it taxes his patience.

Show my wife some love. There's bound to be a doozy coming after that.

A DOOZY WAS not what he would have expected from Kermit Hamrick when the man first came to his door and introduced himself. They lived at opposite corners of the neighborhood that had begun as a nineteenth-century logging camp, but Price only knew Hamrick and his wife by sight.

"Look," he said, "I've heard you're a decent guy. I'm going to be honest here. I'm in the middle of a divorce and my wife is in a bad way. I thought that maybe, with you right down the block like this, you might check up on her every once in a while? Make sure everything is okay?"

Price had been impressed by the man, around his age, who explained that his wife had a prescription drug problem. Deputy Price was not surprised by this. The majority of addiction problems these days came from pharmaceutical drugs. Hamrick assured him that he did not intend to make the pills an issue in the divorce, nor did he want to get his ex in trouble.

Hamrick was afraid she was going to try to do herself in. Guilt was all over the guy.

"She's not a bad woman," Hamrick had said. "She's just in pain and I can't…well, I'm just a reminder. I can't be around anymore. It's all been said at this point, but somebody needs to do something. Somebody needs to stop in every once in a while."

I can't be around. Price wondered what the guy did. Whatever it was, he still seemed honest and sincere. Price said he'd look in on her.

He waited for over a week before he made the stop, a couple of hours before he had to be on afternoon duty. He wore his uniform, to keep it professional.

She came to the door in a pair of sweats and a t-shirt. She looked rumpled and sleepy. She cracked the door partway open and held a cigarette out from her face, her elbow propped on her side.

"What?" she asked.

"Mrs. Hamrick?"

"Not for long. Call me Betty."

"Ma'am, I'm your neighbor, Tommy Price. I live over on Adams? I work for Sheriff Johnson?" He grinned, gesturing to his clothing.

"And?"

"Well, this is just courtesy call. Check in with my neighbors, maybe get to know the neighborhood a little better."

"Sorry," she said, "not really interested," and started to close the door.

"Uh, wait." He held up his hand. "Please."

She kept the door open a crack, peeking out, and for the first time, Price noted that she had pretty eyes.

"Look, if I'm being honest here, I should tell you that your husband asked me to stop, make sure you were doing alright."

She rolled her eyes. "Oh, fucking great, so I guess he's trying to catch me at something?" She yanked the door back open. "Well, come on in! Check all the drawers! I got nothing."

"No, no, ma'am, nothing like that, really. Honestly, I'm just here as your neighbor. See if there is anything you might need that I can help you with."

"I can't talk today. Come back tomorrow." She closed the door.

"AND THAT'S JUST how it happened," says Wally. "I got down here on my knees begging her to stay and she ran me over with my own truck. She just went crazy, plum crazy. I never seen the like."

Price can hear the ambulance siren now. Time for the question of the hour.

"Mr. Stevens, do you wish to press assault charges against your wife?"

This appears to take him aback, and for a moment, Price sees the wheels spinning, the eyes darting, weighing the possibilities. Finally, Wally says, "No…no, I expect not."

Right, thinks Price, who would take care of your pathetic, crippled ass?

"Okay then, I'm going to go hear your wife's statement. The ambulance'll get you all squared away."

"If that woman casts aspersions, don't you believe her!"

THE NEXT DAY, Betty Hamrick opened the door in a pair of Daisy Dukes and a tied burgundy half-blouse, a dainty gold loop dangling from her navel and dreamcatcher earrings. She was a little thing for sure, maybe five feet, with straight black hair hanging around her shoulders.

She pushed open the door and he walked in. She gestured to the couch. "You want some coffee, neighbor?"

Before he could formulate a "Sure," Price had to watch the way the bottom of her ass hung out of the shorts as she walked toward the kitchen. She was tiny, but she looked like she was packing dynamite that was ready to explode. He wondered if he should have refused the coffee, but it was hard to help someone without getting to know them, even if they were incredibly sexy.

"It's just like that self-righteous fucker," Betty said, handing him a cup and sitting on the other end of the gray couch with the extra-wide armrests. "Sorry, I'm outta cream and sugar." She laughed. "Sending a fucking cop over. Like I'm some delinquent. Him, over there in that trailer with that whore secretary sucking his dick."

There it is, Price thought.

"He's gone out of his way to be the reasonable one, you know, letting me have the house. And now, in his twisted pothole-fixing mind, he's replaced himself with you. Send over a big strong policeman to keep control of the delinquent."

She waved her arms in the air, agitated, in the way he'd seen other jonesing pill heads, even Junior in the months following his car accident.

"And here you are, big strong policeman!" The tone was one of exasperation, not enthusiasm, and for a minute, Price felt sympathy for her. She seemed lost, alone, and yes, he could see the pain there, lingering behind those brown eyes.

"I heard he's planning to run for the House of Delegates or some shit." She looked away, her eyes glassing over.

"Ma'am. Betty." He caught himself and moved a little forward on the couch. "I don't want to intrude."

"Don't be silly," she said. "I'm not complaining. It *is* nice to have a big, strong man here. Are you married, big, strong man?"

"Tommy," he said

"Tommy," she continued. "Are you married?"

"Engaged." He smiled.

"Bet she's a real nice girl." Betty said. "Real pretty."

"Yeah, she is." Price realized it was the first time he'd thought of Laura in quite a while, and the image he conjured of her—in her sundress, in soft focus with the light behind her—stood in sharp contrast to the exposed curve of Betty's breast.

"Hmm, don't do it." She took a long sip from her cup, looking at him over the rim. Then, she set the cup down on the coffee table and leaned toward him. "You ever step out, deputy?" She raised her eyebrows. "On that woman?"

"No." Price laughed. He marveled at her magnetism.

"Because I just had an evil idea."

"No, Betty, I don't think so."

Her eyes got even bigger and she scooted closer. "So, you know my evil idea?"

He did indeed. He began to think about an excuse to get out of there. Funny, how they eluded him.

Betty reached out and touched the knot of the dark brown tie that rested on his beige shirt. "Because, you know, I've always had a thing for a guy in uniform." She leaned in closer, whispering. "For a guy with *power.*"

"It's not a good idea, Mrs. Hamrick," Price said, conscious of her hand on his chest.

"Oh! We're back to that, are we?" She scooted close enough for her knee to touch his thigh. "You see, I'm thinking, if he wants to send over a big, strong man, he'd better be ready for what I want to do with that big, strong man."

Damn right, thought Price, and just as he realized he'd actually thought those words, she kissed him. As soon as he kissed her back, she swung her leg over his lap, straddling him, thrusting her tongue into his mouth, and guiding his hand under her blouse as she gyrated on his lap. Price could feel desperation in every move. He liked it.

She pulled her lips slowly from his and tilted her head back, looking at him with an ornery expression.

"You know," she said, reaching down and stroking his hard-on through his pants, "maybe we can work out a little arrangement."

Price's mind became suspicious. His erection did not.

"And what would that be?"

"Well, I was just thinking," she whispered, her lips brushing against his ear. "I'll just bet you could get your hands on all kinds of fun stuff that the cops confiscate. I bet there's all kind of goodies in that evidence room that no one would miss."

He picked her up off his lap, deposited her on the couch, and stood, trying to smooth his trousers.

"No," he said, turning toward the door.

She got up and ran in front of him. "But you're a cop," she said, putting her hands to his chest. "You know where all the good stuff is." She slid her hands down to his beltline. "I could *really* make it worth your while."

Price reached up to remove her hands, but they were already off of him and she was backing off toward the hallway, his handcuffs dangling from her extended finger.

"Come get 'em," she said.

"Come on, Betty. Let me have those." He took a step forward and she squealed, turning to run down the hall past the kitchen, and then he was chasing her and she was laughing as she tried to close the bedroom door and he pushed his way through. He grabbed her as she tried to keep the cuffs from him, giggling all the while, and now he was getting mad, and he still had a hard-on, and she was hot and alone, and he pushed her down, bent her over the edge of the bed, pressing into her back with his forearm, reaching under her and pulling out the arm that held the cuffs. And then he was bending that arm behind her and pulling out the other, affixing the cuffs behind her back. Her breath came fast and deep now and she gasped with the clasp of the tight cuffs. With his hand still pressed into her back, he reached his other hand under her waist and unsnapped the shorts. Betty moaned into the mattress as he yanked them down and jerked them loose from around her ankles.

The moan sent him off his head. She shouldn't be enjoying it. She needed to be punished. A pill whore who needed a dose of reality, to see what happens when you try to extort a cop.

He pushed her face harder into the mattress, kicking her legs out to the side like a perp against the side of the cruiser, unfastening his belt and pants. Just before they fell, he thought to grab his 9-millimeter from the holster and lay it on the bed next to her squirming body. He plunged himself into her, pulling her cuffed hands toward him, bending her backwards from the shoulders and forcing a strong grunt from her lips. He grabbed a handful of her hair and yanked her head backward, driving so hard into her that she slid further onto the bed, her feet coming up off the floor. And now her grunts were sounding a little too much like pleasure and he reached his hand around her neck, squeezing, until her breaths were the sound of air escaping from a balloon.

He could feel her legs quaking and quivering and her feet flailing around through the air as his world went white and he thought, for a moment, that he experienced the divine.

"TRIED TO SHOW me a little love?" Trudy laughs, aiming her next words straight at the driveway. "Is that what they call it when you take your wife by the neck and shove her face in your crotch and say 'suck it?'"

The paramedics are here now, trying to assess the damage to Wally as he yells, "Don't believe it, officers!"

"Thirty years!" Trudy exclaims at elevated decibels. "Thirty years and he *still* ain't figured out a better way of asking for a blowjob!"

"I'm a Christian man!"

Price turns to look at that one. The paramedics are laughing. To the side of Trudy, Pete is barely holding it together, waiting to see if he can "believe it."

Price *is* having a little problem with hearing the word blowjob coming out of friendly old Trudy's mouth, the mouth that so often makes everyone in the diner laugh as she pours the coffee. The sweet older lady that serves him his meat loaf every Tuesday and country fried steak on Thursday.

Now somehow, Price needs to incorporate blowjobs onto that menu, and he is having trouble with it. With all these new facets of himself at the forefront of his thoughts, he is struggling to work in new wrinkles from others.

"Blowjob!" says Trudy. "Blowjob, blowjob, blowjob, blowjob, blowjob!"

AFTER THE INCIDENT with Betty, Price stood in front of the bathroom mirror at work and wondered who the hell he was. The look she'd given him afterward, that she'd given to the gun, had stayed with him. He hadn't said anything before he left. And now, uncertainty nagged at his reflection. Had he gone too far? He and Laura had played with the cuffs. He figured every cop had. But it never felt like *that*. It always felt like play-acting. He would never be able to do that with Laura again. She would never understand. He could never go that far. His reflection steeled itself.

Betty Hamrick was just another pill head. She wouldn't cause trouble. If her ex ever found out and he was in the

House of Delegates, he could make trouble but it seemed like he was looking to put her behind. Price wondered how far Junior would go for him. It took him back to where such thoughts always took him, to Hot Dog Sam, the first time he'd understood that some lines get crossed. It took a while to get that black man and his hot dog cart out of the county. He was stubborn, kept insisting he had the right to set up in public spaces and kept accusing them of working for Trevelton restaurateurs. They were, in some way, Price knew, but he wasn't getting paid anything other than his salary. Junior had let him be part of the last visit and Price landed a few punches. After that, Junior told him he'd always have his back. Damned if some pill head was going to ruin that. If he needed to shut her up, he knew how to do it. He knew where the drugs were. Every cop knew where the drugs were. That wasn't the problem, of course. The problem was getting them without anyone knowing, which meant a clandestine visit to the local source.

Aside from the small operations that popped up occasionally, there was one major trafficker in this area, a biker out on Jackson Road who ran his own garage and owned a strip club on Route 12. He must have had family ties somewhere because he was allowed to go about his business unimpeded. That, or it might have been the threat of reprisal represented by his motorcycle club. In any case, Price could just go out there for a "car appointment." Problem solved.

But over the next two days, the possibility of giving someone else power over him, namely the dealer, gave him pause. And he couldn't quit thinking about taking Betty. Taking her. The idea of a woman ready to do anything for the drugs was one thing, but it struck him a lot like paying for sex, which Tommy Price had never done-- never. Taking

Betty had been mystical, powerful, as if he was about to break through to an unknown part of himself, wild and free, a beast of tooth and claw and blood and sex, of violence and rape. Betty's grunts and moans rang in his ears, primal cries he couldn't get out of his head.

A couple nights after it happened, he pulled some station duty and ended up beating the hell out of a smart-ass kid in the holding cell with soap in a sock. He stopped when he realized his dick was getting hard, and left quickly, embarrassed. He slipped into the bathroom to relieve himself, but as he imagined Betty bent over the bed, images of the kid, wincing with the soap-blows, kept mixing in until he realized it was the boy bent over the bed. His dick withered in his grasp and his anger grew. He knew what he wanted.

The next day, a mere eight hours before Trudy Stevens would run over her husband, Price returned to Betty Hamrick's door.

THE STROBE OF the ambulance's lights flash orange on the porch where the story is becoming clear of how Wallace Stevens, after his lewd act, pursued his wife through the mobile home, swinging the buckle end of his belt when she escaped from his grasp.

"So, how did it get to this?" asks Price, waving his arm toward the driveway.

"Well," Trudy says, "I grabbed the first set of keys I saw and hightailed it out the front door. I was glad they was the truck keys, 'cause I knew he wouldn't harm his precious truck. I ran over there and locked myself in and he came over and started banging on the window. When I saw his dick was out, that was it. I started the truck to get out of here. Well, he says, 'You ain't going nowhere!' and runs out there and lays down in the driveway like some kind of pathetic pervert protestor with his pecker hanging out." A wisp of steam rises from the top of her head in the chilly November air.

"Okay Trudy, I get it, but if you ran him over, and he's still laying there, well, how did the truck get back in front of the garage?

"Oh, I wanted to make sure I got him."

At this, Deputy Pete Beck cannot contain himself and exhales with a loud honk. Price gives the kid a look.

"It was the dick hanging out that sent me over the edge, Tommy. I was aiming for his dick. I hope I hit it." She leans to the side slightly and raises her voice. "I hope I broke that thing into three pieces, you old pervert!"

"Eh, you missed it by a few inches, Trudy."

"Too bad. Thirty years he's been doing that shit to me."

"I don't think he'll be doing it again."

"It's why a body would put up with it. That's the question."

BETTY ONLY OPENED the door a crack.

"You bring me something?"

"No."

"Then get outta here." She started to close the door, but Price got a foot in and pushed the rest of the way into the living room. Betty began beating at him with her fists.

"Get the fuck outta here!"

"No," he said.

He took hold of her arms as she swung at him and twisted them behind her back. He pushed her across the room and face down over the extra-wide armrest of the sofa. He cuffed her like before. She wasn't struggling anymore. Price thought she might be stoned. All the better. He set his gun on the back of the sofa. Then, he sodomized her.

When the light had again faded from his vision, the ecstasy once more floating off into the irretrievable, he freed her from the cuffs, again with no words. She gathered her sweatpants and panties from the floor and started toward the bathroom. Before she closed the door, she spoke out into the hallway.

"I've got my phone in here with me. If you're not out of here in five minutes, I'm calling 911." She closed the door and then reopened it enough to speak through the crack. "And if you ever come here again without something for my head—a lot of somethings for my head—I'll do the same."

After he left, Price pulled off the road and stared into the trees until it felt like they were moving in, surrounding him. She had threatened to report him. Would Junior really have his back? Maybe a paid leave until everything blows over, like when Miller shot the meth-head last year? Price knew how rape cases usually went. He figured he could beat it but wanted to keep his job. It would definitely be best if it all stayed under the radar. He considered the local paper, a conservative publication. They had taken Miller's side, running a feature on how local departments were better able to protect the public because of the assault weapons, body armor, and military vehicles that they were receiving from the federal government in response to the terrorism threat. Rumor had it that the county was getting a gunboat.

"SO, TRUDY, I guess the question is, do you want to press assault charges?"

Trudy looks out into the night where the ambulance has just departed. Since Price already knows the answer, his thoughts drift back to Betty, to Laura, his intended. She must never find out about this. He remembers how, after Hot Dog Sam, Junior had told him, "Ain't going to be no trouble. It's a new day, Tommy, my boy. We're the good guys." He can't allow that judgment to change, whether it's for hot dog vendors, teenage vandals, or pill-head sluts with a hurt look. She knew what she was doing.

"Oh hell, Tommy," Trudy says, "I'm gonna have to put up with enough whining as it is. I'll torture him for a few weeks just to make sure he gets the message."

Price puts a hand on her shoulder and smiles. It makes him feel fatherly and, in a way, excused. "You got some spunk there, Trudy. You let me know if you have trouble with him and let *us* get him back in line, alright?" Price hopes that maybe he'll get that chance, someday.

Trudy still watches from the porch as the deputies walk back to their cruisers. Pete isn't letting go yet, no guffaws or knee-slapping. He is playing it cool. Out of the side of his mouth, he says, "I didn't know the old girl had it in her."

"I'd have thought you wouldn't be surprised what people got in em at this point."

Pete looks up as Trudy steps back into the trailer. As he opens the cruiser door, he looks back at Price, nodding toward the trailer. "You think she gives good head?"

Price grins at him and that seems to satisfy Pete for the moment. As the other deputy drives off, Price puts away his notebook and thinks briefly that it might be fun to punch

Pete in the face just for being an idiot, just for the fun of seeing his expression.

He drives back out Corwin Road and turns north toward Trevelton on Route Twelve. Passing downtown Dogleg Bend, he imagines her, just up the hill from there. He is going to have to insure her silence. He knows that. But there are things that need to be figured out first; calculations to be made and weighed.

Everybody knows where the drugs are. That isn't the problem.

How to Get Away from the World

AT SOME POINT in your life, you might find yourself ready to run away from the world.

Many people do. Many people get to a place where they say, "I can't take it anymore," and then just seemingly drop off into the dark corners of the Earth. It's much more common than you might think. You might be, say, a shoe salesman who finally admits that he hates feet, or possibly a chef who has seen one too many soufflés fall. You might even be an ex-employee of the Central Intelligence Agency, someone who's seen too much, someone who needs to hide, someone who, well. You get the picture. You could be that guy. Or any one of those guys, or girls. You could be that girl. That girl chef.

In the midst of this crisis, you might remember once seeing a picture of the Earth at night with its spider webs of light and noticing that there existed only one significant dark place on the whole east coast of the United States. If you then consulted an online map, you might zoom in on that area and discover that there is a town called Dogleg Bend, West Virginia. You will most likely think to yourself, no shit? There's really a place called Dogleg Bend, West Virginia? And once you come to grips with this fact, it is likely that you'll assume that it doesn't get much farther out than that.

Now, you will imagine your new home, out there in that big dark patch, away from everything and everyone, solar and wind-powered, nothing that stands out, a small and simple place, off the grid. And you might think, here. Here it is. The place where you can get away from all the undercooked Beef Wellingtons, the vastly underestimated problem of foot bromhidrosis, the uncomfortable implications of a hostile debriefing.

At this juncture, you will need the services of a local realtor. Search for an independent agent, unaffiliated with any national chains. The time has come for you to put into use those large piles of cash that you have been hiding away all these years. Hopefully, you remembered those large piles of cash, because they are instrumental in maintaining your anonymity.

ANONYMITY, NATURALLY, IS crucial to your whole purpose. You cannot afford to gamble that your whereabouts will become known, for obvious reasons. To this end, you will need to take care of several things.

All cell phones, for instance, can be easily tracked. You will, therefore, have to purchase "burners." These cheap phones can be fraudulently registered, used temporarily, and thrown away. You will use these for all your communications and it will complicate any attempts by sinister agencies to monitor you in this way.

For purchases, especially purchases of land onto which you plan to disappear, it would be extremely helpful to have a false identity. There are plenty of good identity thieves out there. You can find one for a reasonable price at your local college's freshman dorms. There, you will make the acquaintance of a pale, spectacled lad named Nelson Boyd, who will take your picture in front of a blue sheet that he hangs over top of a beer-bong dangling from a coat hook and a World of Warcraft poster. He will then provide you with a new social security number, birth certificate, and a valid driver's license.

Beyond the cell phone issue and the process of obtaining a false identity, it must be noted that many current vehicle models are equipped with GPS units which can be tracked anywhere on the planet. Before travelling to your new locale, you will have to trade down to an older model vehicle so that your movements will not be logged.

WHEN SEARCHING FOR an independent real estate man in Trevelton, West Virginia, it is likely that you will end up with a realtor named Wilbur Smith, and you might say to yourself, "No shit? Wilbur? Really?" But Wilbur, despite his "down home" manner, will turn out to be quite the dynamo, and after only a few weeks of phone calls, will call to tell you he's found the perfect property, set in Bergen County but not part of any municipality. You will ask if there is an access road and he will assure you that there is.

"And some level terrain?" you'll inquire.

"Sure as you're born," he'll say.

"Because I want to build," you'll remind him, laying your index finger on the blueprints there on the kitchen table, as if Wilbur could see their self-sustaining beauty through the phone.

"Oh it's level, alright," he'll say. "'Course, you're gonna have to clear out some."

"And it's not near any mountaintop removal sites?" you'll ask, as you glance again at the horrific picture still on your computer screen, also on your kitchen table.

"Nearest one of those is twenty miles."

"Because I don't want any water problems."

"Well, there ain't no city water out in them parts, so you're gonna have to dig, as far as that goes," Wilbur will say. "But there shouldn't be any problems with the water there. What do you think? Want to come have a look-see?"

"Okay, but my phone number has changed."

"Again?"

After you've given Wilbur your new number, you will want to go out and buy a bottle of wine for a quiet celebration. It is somewhat possible that your new forged driver's license will be rejected by the young cashier with the tattoos. Should this situation arise, *do not* attempt to use this identity for purchasing your property. And, regardless of what you might have heard about the quality of his forgery work, *do not* go to the sketchy Chechnyan at the corner of Wilson and 3rd. He is under surveillance. You should know this. You're a shoe salesman. Woman. You're a shoe saleswoman.

SO, WHAT WILL probably happen now is that, after many pitfalls and travails on the road, you'll get to Trevelton and meet Wilbur, who wears a plaid dress-shirt and jeans. After some confusion as to your change in name, he'll drive you out past a Walmart and a Motel 6 to the little town of Dogleg Bend, where he'll turn his green Jeep Cherokee west onto a secondary road which isn't much more than a tar-chip surface. You'll be twisting back and forth on that road for some miles before you turn onto another dirt road, left nameless here, of course, to avoid disclosing your whereabouts.

"Yes sir, this is God's Country up here," Wilbur is likely to say, and you'll be hard-pressed to disagree. You'll look out over those rounded mountains covered with early spring green and feel how you could lose yourself in that ancient bosom. You'll gaze out on the endless mounds of rising earth and be able to see them, as they were when they were young and jagged. You'll be so struck with this primeval majesty that, when you come to the property in question, all will seem magical: the bluebirds, the raccoon, the trees. Everything will seem so magical that you are likely to overlook what seem to be small problems with your plan.

DO NOT DO THIS.

Pulling as far into the woods as he can in his Jeep, Wilbur will probably say, "Well, there's a bit of an access here, anyway. Obviously, you'll have to remove a few more trees. But we can walk from here."

A ten-minute walk uphill through the woods will bring you to a beautiful flat area that overlooks the mountains to the east. It will look like the perfect place for your dream home, and you will be able to picture the sun rising on your mountain hideaway. A stand of aspens on the other side of the clearing with their bumpy greenish bark will promise afternoon shade and you will notice, in the middle of that flat area, rising up through the new shoots of weeds like the back of a giant turtle submerged in the mud, a mound of rock that stretches some twenty yards from side to side.

"What about that rock?" you'll ask.

"Oh, a little dynamite should take care of that rock," he says.

At that instant, a deer will run out in front of you, bat its eyelashes, paw at the ground and seem to welcome you to your new home.

Don't listen to it. It's a traitorous beast. And it only wants your corn.

IT IS LIKELY by now, after your fifth burner phone, that you will come to the realization that all the calls you have made have been to established, monitorable lines and recognize this for what it is: a threat to your secrecy. The only solution in this case would be to make sure all your phone contacts use burners as well. Wilbur Smith will refuse to do this. So will your mom.

It is also likely that you will already have had to replace the engine in your older model vehicle when it "threw a rod," and you may find yourself considering the option of returning to a newer model. Again, buying a GPS-equipped vehicle would sacrifice your privacy unless you were able to purchase it with a false identity, but seeing as how that identity did not pass the scrutiny of a convenience store clerk with tattoos, this will hardly seem a viable option.

In fact, with the property sale imminent, you will most likely have to resign yourself to Plan B, which would be to use your real identity and cross your fingers that it all flies under the radar. While you're at it, just go ahead and get a new car…and a smart phone.

HOPEFULLY, YOU WILL have heeded the earlier warnings. Hopefully, you don't buy into the deer's bullshit. But if you do, here is what awaits you:

You will likely take Wilbur Smith's advice and enlist the aid of the "Miller Boys," your heretofore unknown neighbors who live "a couple miles down thataway." Boys, you will discover, is a relative term. These two middle-aged brothers, who arrive in an International pickup truck so old it still has a choke control, will offer to remove the trees for the access road and the large rock in the middle of your level spot for a couple thousand dollars. Little do you realize at this point that you are paying for a party of beer, chainsaws, and dynamite. While the brothers manage to clear all the trees necessary to get vehicles to the site, they leave the knotted stumps and fallen logs lying off to the side, a game of pickup sticks awaiting a colossal eight-year-old.

And as for the rock, well, you get to witness some of that particular debacle yourself before Carl, the oldest of the "boys," the one with the AC/DC tattoo, says, "You know, I think that rock goes clear down!"

He will pause and rub his stubbly chin before saying, "You might need to get some guys in here who know what they're doing better'n me."

A sudden but brief panic will seize you. A professional demolition team. How much will that cost? What red flags will *that* raise? You are too far in to back out now. But the budget you have is already strained and going to a bank for a loan is like shooting off a flare for the powers who wish to find you. Much of your plan depends upon getting a speedy start on your house. Now, you will have to stay longer in the creepy Motel 6 by the Walmart, which is going to drain you of even more cash.

"You know," Carl will say, "you got plenty of level space here to bring in a trailer."

It's a possibility you haven't considered. You'll see it as a way to buy some time.

"'Course, we'll have to take out some more trees to get it in here," Carl will add.

It is at this moment, this *exact* moment, that you will look out over your new access "road," and formulate the following words in your mind: My God, there's no electricity out here. How much is that going to cost?

All because you listened to that damnable deer.

SOMETIME AFTER THE trailer has been put in place, after the electricity but before the plumbing, you will decide to begin moving your things in. Carl Miller will mention that he and his brother will "be out four-wheeling later" and offer to "stop by" to visit with a couple beers, just as a way of welcoming you to the neighborhood. Understanding that you may need their help again, you will be tempted to say, "Sure!" This is inadvisable.

With the involvement of the electric company, state government, OnStar, Apple, Microsoft, AT&T, and DirecTV, the grid is now fully aware of your activities and location. It is doubly important, at this point, that you tend to appearances. The small details can save the day, as any good chef should know…as any good woman chef should know…oh, the hell with it. You're not a woman…seriously…even if you are.

So, after that first "four-wheeler" party, when ten all-terrain vehicles laden with coolers of alcohol come bursting out of the woods like a swarm of giant buzz-roar bugs, and everyone sits around in front of your trailer drinking, and Carl and some guy named "One-Hand" (no, you don't know why—he has both hands) get into an all-out brawl, you may feel like you made a mistake letting it happen in the first place.

No, no one expects you to listen to any of the warnings at this point.

ED BREWSTER, THE dowser, will likely complicate things further when he tells you that your trailer is sitting on solid rock and that your well will have to be dug some 200 yards away and pipe laid to the trailer. He assures you the same will be true of your septic system. The Miller boys will volunteer to do these jobs for a reasonable price, pulling you further into their world, entangling you in a personal relationship, the quickest way to undermine your efforts to stay hidden. This will be clearly evident when the second four-wheeler party takes you by surprise, despite your culinary training.

This time, Carl will likely bring along two new things: some of his daddy's "'shine" and his little sister, Norma, and twelve muddy people will come barging into your trailer hideaway wanting to see how the plumbing is working out. Not surprisingly, someone will see the documents that you saved to write your tell-all book lying on your kitchen table and start asking you uncomfortable questions about…well…secret recipes and stuff. You will gather up your papers quickly and claim that they are all your own inventions, but everyone will look at you funny for a long time.

That is, until the jar has made a couple rounds of the room, and then everyone will be clapping you on the back again.

Norma, a rather plain but not unattractive woman of around 30, will be shy and withdrawn at the beginning of the evening, but as the night wears on, you will find her snuggled up under your armpit on the couch, looking up at you with big eyes and saying, "Is it true you were a secret agent?" And to your horror, the following morning you will remember telling her all about clandestine missions in Afghanistan, Hong Kong, and the Ukraine.

Okay, so you're not a chef either. That's dispensed with, too. Another fallen soufflé.

Two other memories, equally horrifying, will emerge that morning. You, standing on the bed, showing Norma a new dance move that you call the "Sketchy Chechnyan," and then something else, something soft, warm, intimate, and delicious. Something stupid. Oh, so stupid.

SOMETIMES, YOU JUST have to admit you aren't up to the task.

Some weeks after that second party, you will find yourself at the Walmart outside of Dogleg Bend when you will feel eyes upon you. Turning, you will see a child staring at you who then tugs on his mother's shirt and says, "It's the secret agent, Mommy."

Having admitted utter failure in dropping off the grid, you will now have to bring yourself to face other problems. Like the fact that your entire tenure in the CIA consisted of sitting in a risk assessment office in Virginia, running vast amounts of intercepted international communications through voice and print recognition software and sending the data on to an algorithmic team for analysis.

So, no, you aren't a secret agent either.

But still, it isn't completely out of the question that someone might need the information you possess, that you could be tracked and extracted, debriefed under the cruelest conditions, and murdered with no one the wiser.

Well, maybe it is...

Or maybe it isn't, because there will certainly appear to be murder in the eyes of Mr. Franklin Miller the morning he knocks on your trailer door and asks about your intentions regarding his daughter, Norma. Carl and Bill will be standing behind him, alternately looking earnestly at their father and sternly at you.

Franklin Miller will say, "I don't care if ya are trained to kill," and grip his shotgun with white knuckles.

When this happens, aside from the fact that you might feel all of your plans unraveling and that this all might be reminding you of the plot of an Andy Griffith Show somewhere from your distant past, you will likely feel a strong impulse to offer to marry Norma.

SO, THERE YOU'LL be now, living in a trailer with a woman named Norma, and asking yourself how it ever came to this. Whatever happened to your secret bungalow, solar-powered, hidden from all the world? Whatever happened to your meditative self-sufficiency? And at times like this, you will find yourself ruminating on what prompted you to go into hiding in the first place.

What did you witness while you were there at that non-descript desk in that non-descript brick building in Virginia?

Certainly nothing specifically scary. Unbridled stupidity and hubris? Dubious goals and dubious means of attaining them? Perverted priorities? Circumventing the Constitution? Withheld cooperation? Politics? Wasn't working in this secretive, bungling bureaucracy just enough to drive you paranoid into the night, to a mountain hideaway where you could just cut yourself off from all of it, deny you were ever a part of it, and wait for the bastards to bring it all to ruin?

Can anybody really blame me for that?

Shit.

Sometimes, we just have to admit that no matter where we go, the Millers will find us. Sometimes, we have to admit that they're probably the only ones really looking.

But, as you will discover, the Millers are alright. Everything will work in your trailer, despite the giant stone turtle burrowed in your front yard. You'll continue to spin wild yarns about your adventures as a secret agent as you keep every four-wheeler party crowd enraptured, and yes, every time they will ask to see your old CIA identification badge, and they'll pass it around the room and marvel at it.

Eventually, you will confess to Norma, only to find she already knows your secret. In this way, Norma will be a marvelous partner, one who knows you well, and you will be surprised and delighted to discover she is a college graduate. At night, she will read you Robert Frost poems, and your relationship will grow deeper over time. Your new mother-in-law, Retha, will bring you canned vegetables during the winter. Bill will supply you with fresh meats during hunting season. Carl will bring you a puppy.

Even the intimidating old moonshiner Franklin will come by and teach you how to put in a garden, and you will plant your first rows of corn.

And the deer will have his due.

Suicidal Gods

I

I ONCE KISSED Dewey Burke. That's not something I brag on generally, nor does it rank among the most pleasant experiences of my life, but we were half-drunk and, when you get down to it, I actually kissed him twice. We both agreed that the first one wasn't done with much enthusiasm, and that if we really wanted to know if we were gay or not, we needed to push the experience a little further. So, we went at that second one more seriously, and when it was over, and Dewey said, "I love ya, brother Ned, but that just don't feel right." I found myself in complete agreement. When I look back on it, the experience was like when you pick up your can of beer, take a swig, and discover a cigarette butt in the can.

It's not surprising that it came to that point. We *had* been called fags through middle and high school. I mean, we'd had girlfriends, and I don't think any of those people really thought we were gay. It's just the only way they had to deal with how close me and Dewey were, so they made fun of it. We never really cared, but sometimes, when you hear things over and over, even as a joke, you start to wonder.

And even though neither one of our peckers grew during our experiment, it was clear that something else moved, inside. It was like when we were ten and walked across the trestle over Diggers Creek. It ran forty feet or so above the water. We felt bigger when it was over, like we had defied gravity. The kiss was something like that. I wonder sometimes if that was where all the trouble started. It seemed like, after that, we just completely lost our patience for bullshit.

DEWEY AND I grew up in West Virginia, just north of Dogleg Bend in Bergen County. We were fortunate. Most of the homes, with the exception of the ones closer to town, were pretty spread out. If you had another kid living within a mile of you, then you were lucky. Dewey and I lived within fifty yards of each other right from the beginning. Since our moms didn't talk, we didn't get to know each other until we were around four.

Dewey lived with his mom, Deborah, above The Henhouse, a strip club that sat along Route Twelve at the Jackson Road turnoff. She was a stripper in the early days, but later, she managed the place. The Henhouse was a plain-looking, stucco rectangle. A set of rusty iron steps ascended to a covered walk that stretched along the back of the building to the apartment doors. On the front of the building beside the name was a blue wooden rooster painted to look like he was winking at you and giving you the ol' thumbs-up with his weathered feathers. Deborah maintained a relationship with the sign's namesake, Rooster, who owned the place, so she got a good deal on the apartment upstairs. Back then, she'd always say, "Listen boys, I may love him, but there's no way I wanna live with him." Rooster was not Dewey's dad. We never knew who Dewey's dad was.

Rooster lived out past my house, further out on Jackson Road, which followed the natural gaps in the hills, flat and grassy, like a misty snake laid out in the morning sun. Several small farms were out that way and Rooster owned one of them, though he didn't really work it. He was a member of a motorcycle club that I won't mention, and he owned a garage that he built on that property, where he worked on people's cars.

I lived about fifty yards from The Henhouse. All that sat between Dewey and me was a gravel parking lot, a chain-link fence overgrown with vines, a strip of woods, and Diggers Creek, which ran through it. I remember the first day we saw each other through those plants and trees, a moment suspended in time, separated from everything else.

I lived in a double-wide, set up on blocks for those times that Diggers Creek swelled, with my mom and pop and younger sister, Jenny. Pop drove for a trucking company. I don't know which one, or even what he hauled. All I know is that he was gone a lot until the day he hurt his back and retired to the recliner in the living room with his beer. I was six years old then, and any desire to connect with my father disappeared when I discovered he wasn't the man I'd imagined he was. He was a cranky, mean, lazy bastard who beat on me and killed my dog. After he went on disability, Mom went to work in the cafeteria at my elementary school.

It looks foreboding, I know, one kid with the alcoholic father, the other raised by an ex-stripper, both headed for trouble, but it wasn't that bad. My mom may not have liked her, but Dewey's mom was okay. She'd convinced Rooster to connect the two apartments and gave Dewey the far bedroom over the kitchen so the bar noise wouldn't keep him up at night, and she made sure he had a computer and a PlayStation. My folks never had the money for that stuff, what with the cable bill and Pop's beer to pay for.

Maybe it wasn't fancy, but kids have a way of compensating. For me and Dewey, when we were little, it was the woods and critters that filled the empty parts of us, first that little strip by the creek, and then later branching out into the fields and hills on either side of Jackson Road. We built forts, played war, dreamed of tree houses, caught garter snakes and salamanders, made trails and jumps for our bicycles and skateboards.

No other kids our age lived nearby, so when we weren't in the woods, we were on Dewey's PlayStation or computer. Mom didn't have the energy to fight it anymore and Pop just didn't give a shit. He was one of the first to call us fags. Growing up in West Virginia in the nineties was different than it was for our parents. In their day, everything was a step behind the rest of the world. It still is, but at least now it's connected by more than the television. It's the difference between a peephole and a big window. Me and Dewey gazed out that window a lot.

That's probably another reason for our freak status amongst our peers. While they were listening to country and rap, me and Dewey were downloading Cake, Primus, The Prodigy, Nine Inch Nails, Tool, and music that generally makes country folk nervous. Looking at the world through the computer made some things look normal to us that weren't so normal for the people around us. We were lucky like that, too.

I would never, in a million years, blame my childhood for any of the stuff that happened later, and don't think Dewey would either. We were mostly happy. We didn't know any different. We had each other, and we had Henry Harper.

HENRY HELD LEGENDARY status in Dogleg Bend. There must have been a hundred stories about him floating around, all of which included the fact that he was crazy as a loon. One story said Henry cooperated with the Japanese when he was captured in World War II. Another said he was a devil-worshiper. Another maintained that Henry had a fortune buried on his property, and another that he'd murdered his family. It didn't help that Henry claimed to have tea with a Bigfoot named Old Stinky Joe.

I met Henry for the first time on a Saturday when I went to the grocery store with my mom and sister. One minute, I was begging my mother for Cocoa Krispies instead of Cheerios and Corn Flakes; the next, I was seeing a skinny Santa Claus in baggy jeans, flannel, and suspenders going by the end of the aisle, slow, but sure. Just before he disappeared from sight, he turned and gave me one of the friendliest Santa Claus smiles I'd ever seen. I must have been standing with my mouth hanging open because Mom was rounding the other end of the aisle before I realized she'd moved away.

I didn't believe in Santa at this point, which made it especially disconcerting. The world went topsy-turvy, the twinkling eyes, the bushy white hair bursting out from everywhere on his head, and that toothpick of a body. I walked behind Mom and Jenny, scanning the store for another glimpse until I spied him in the toilet paper aisle. Mom didn't notice I'd stopped. As I watched him pull the big package of single ply from the shelf, I found comfort in the fact that he probably wasn't Santa Claus.

Henry turned around and saw me gawking. He bent over toward me with his hands on his knees. "What's yer name, young feller?"

"Ned Foster."

"C'mon here a sec." He motioned with one of his hands.

I walked over, against the advice of every adult I'd ever known, because there was no way that high and gentle voice held any malice.

He held out his hand for me to shake. "Pleased to meet you, Ned Foster. My name's Henry Harper."

I shook his hand and he said, "Ned, I got a question that's been puzzling me, maybe you can help me with, ya think?"

"I dunno."

"Good answer, young Ned. Now tell me, if you can, what's the sound of one hand clapping?"

I did not know how to answer that. I did not even know how to take that. It struck my nine-year-old brain as ridiculous. I'm sure my mouth dropped open and Henry started chuckling. Then, Mom's voice.

"Ned Foster, you get over here this instant!"

I turned around and rejoined Mom. As we walked, she said, "That man's a crazy old hermit, Ned. You don't be talking to him."

"He asked me what was the sound of one hand clapping."

"See? There you go. Crazy."

I kept thinking about the question. It felt like some code I was supposed to crack, itching under my skin. All through the grocery store, I thought about it, and shortly after, as we walked through the parking lot, I saw him getting into his old blue and white Ford pickup. He looked up and saw me and before I could stop myself, I blurted out, "It don't sound like nothin'!" His laugh rang through the air like the chitter of some extinct bird. He waved and drove off and I didn't see him again for five years.

II

IN THE SPRING of my fourteenth year, J. Allan Davidson, Attorney for Mr. Henry Harper, showed up at my parents' door with a proposal. Mr. Harper needed help around his place with odd jobs over the summer and wanted to hire me. After he'd convinced my parents that no harm would come to me (later I learned that involved money changing hands), the lawyer asked me if I wanted to do it.

There weren't many other jobs around for fourteen-year-olds who wanted to buy video games, so I said, "Can Dewey help, too?" The deal was struck.

Three times a week that summer, Henry would drive down and pick us up and we cleaned junk, trimmed his bushes and backyard, and helped him straighten his crazy artist barn. That was when we learned he was an artist. That was when we learned he flew aerial reconnaissance in the War. That was when we learned he was a Buddhist. That was when we learned about Old Stinky Joe. He had one kooky surprise after another and yet he was so calm, a gentle breeze in a stormy world. Out there at Henry's cabin, it sometimes felt like the mountain was a rock in a stream, and while the rest of the world flowed around and below us, chaotic and violent, we were in the funny/strange Henry reality, safe from it all.

THAT WAS ALSO the summer that me and Dewey both lost our virginity on the very same night.

Rooster convinced Dewey's mom that they needed a weekend at the beach. We all convinced her that it would be okay to leave me and Dewey together. Deborah always trusted too easily.

"It's gonna be alright, Deborah," said Dewey after she explained the rules yet again. He'd called her Deborah since he was five. "Go have fun. We got it under control." He was always a great bullshitter and he put it to work for us that Friday night.

When the bar closed at two, Dewey was waiting out on the apartment landing for the girls to come out back to their cars. I was watching from the window. Dewey had been flirting for a while with Casey, a pretty twenty-two-year-old from Trevelton, blonde and leggy, and when the girls came out, Dewey called down to her.

"Hey Casey, you should come up."

She stopped and turned around. "Oh yeah?" One of the other girls leaned into her and, though we couldn't make out all of what she said, there was a pretty clear "…don't…" floating through the air.

"Yeah," said Dewey. "You should come up and party a little."

"What have you got that a girl like me could party with?"

"Oh, I don't know," said Dewey, smiling. "Maybe a little somethin' somethin'."

This caught her interest and she drifted a step toward the building.

"No, you don't," she said with the sound of someone hoping to be proven wrong. "What is it?"

"Somethin' good. Just come up for a little bit."

She whispered to the girls behind her and approached the stairs. One of the other girls made a half-hearted attempt to grab hold of her shirt, but missed. The other two hightailed it, as if the quicker their departure, the less their involvement.

"Your little friend is here," said Casey when she saw me on the couch.

"Yeah," said Dewey, "we got the place all weekend."

"Oh yeah?" She arched her pretty eyebrows.

She was pissed when Dewey told her we had pot.

"You brought me up here for some lousy weed?"

"No," said Dewey, "we got some beer, too."

"What, the two cans you boys were going to get drunk on tonight?"

Dewey got up and walked into the kitchen. I was speechless, pulled like a magnet to the smooth skin of her thigh emerging from the skirt, the calf, the heels, the plunging neckline. She was beautiful, if you could ignore her inevitable tragedy. I had fallen in love. With all of it.

"You know, Dewey," she said as she took the can, brushing his fingers, "I was hoping maybe you had something a little more fun than beer."

"I do," he said, sitting down and putting his arm around her. "Me!" He grinned.

"Right." She slipped out from under his arm and walked to the window, drawing the curtain back a crack. "Listen boys, I probably shouldn't be here. Deborah would kill me...,"

"I got Oxys," said Dewey.

"Well." She turned, suddenly cheerful, and held her thumb and forefinger out, nearly touching. "I guess I could stay a *little* longer."

Though we'd never dared get into them, we both knew Deborah had a bottle of Oxys in her nightstand from the times Dewey had kyped weed from her stash. But now, Dewey went back to her bedroom and came out with a round, yellow pill in his fingers. He held it out and told Casey to stick out her tongue. She did.

I was getting a little miffed with Dewey. The sight of her tongue accepting the pill had me turned on. In some sort of hero-wannabe way, I was attracted to her lurking, unhappy fate. I just wasn't sure I wanted to contribute to it. And it was getting a little slimy over there. Hanging all over her, encouraging her to drink more, begging little kisses from her giggling lips, telling her not to worry about getting wasted because she could stay there overnight.

Next thing I knew, before my beer was even halfway gone (I still hated the stuff then), Casey just passed out, her head lolling backwards on the couch, her jaw hanging slack. Dewey reached out a finger and prodded her shoulder. "Hey." She didn't move. He poked her again. "Casey." Nothing. Then he pushed his finger into her tit, pressing in slowly until his entire hand was on it, squeezing. "Oh, Ned," he said.

"No, Dewey, c'mon now."

But his hand was already inside her blouse, slowly moving back and forth, rubbing and squeezing, his mouth hanging open in awe, his other arm dancing ecstatically in the air, hand turned backward like some kind of Mexican dancer or bullfighter. "Oh Ned, you gotta…," Casey let out a soft moan and arched her back slightly.

"Stop it, Dewey."

"But she wants it, look."

"No," I said, but I had to look, regardless. Now Dewey's other hand was sneaking up her skirt and he looked like the master criminal. Her breathing quickened and she moaned again. Her eyes were still closed.

"Oh, man, she is wet. She wants us to fuck her, Ned. We have to."

And now I was hard as a rock, painful hard, and it made me feel like a dirtbag. I stood up.

"Dewey, stop it now. I don't know what the fuck's wrong with you. It ain't right."

"I got a finger in there, dude, oh, holy shit." Her pelvis was moving up and down and I'd had enough. I started across the room to make him stop, but I didn't get two steps before her eyes opened and she pushed Dewey's hands slowly from her body. Sitting forward, she looked Dewey in the eye and pointed at me. "*He's* first," she said and stood up, taking my hand in hers and leading me back the hall toward the bedroom.

I looked back and Dewey's mouth was open, a hurt expression on his face. I flipped him the bird.

Later, listening to her in there with Dewey, it occurred to me that maybe I didn't have to give her a pill to contribute to her inevitable doom. When it was all over and Dewey gave her a few more pills, Casey left. At some point, she quit showing up for work and we never saw her again.

LATER THAT SUMMER, we got to explore the trailer up on the hill beside Henry's place when we moved a bunch of rolled-up paintings from his studio in the barn. That trailer was filled with paintings and drawings in every room. A queen-size bed frame and mattress leaned against the living room wall. Henry said the bed came with the trailer, which he bought used.

Every time we went in there, we were an hour exploring. There were some wild pictures and we'd get all smoked up and look for the craziest. One of our favorites was the shadowy hulk of Old Stinky Joe coming out of the woods. Henry appreciated our interest, and one day gave us each a painting, framed and everything. He called mine a mandala and said that if I could ever picture it exactly in my mind, it would help me remember the deep secrets that belonged to me alone.

I didn't take it back home. Pop would never let up about it. I gave it to Dewey to hold onto for me, and he hung it in his living room. Deborah liked it.

THAT FALL, EVERYTHING changed, or at least the TV said it did, when two jumbo jets crashed into the World Trade Center in New York.

At first, me and Dewey were sucked into it, like everyone was, but as it went along, the volume just increased. We'd seen people riled up about different stuff before, but the one thing those times had in common was that they were over, sometimes in just days, sometimes weeks. Rarely would they last more than a month. But this one just got louder. Pop would scream about how we needed to kill all them Arabs. Of course, he was doing that right from the beginning. Everybody was an expert, and everyone was afraid.

"I'll tell ya," Henry said, "fear is a terrible thing, fellers. Makes you shut out the scary truth and believe the pretty lies." He pointed at his chest. "It goes deep. It hides, makes you angry, embarrassed. You could go inside yourself and dig them fears out for years, boys, but there's still more, buried deeper. The hard questions, that's the only way to deal with fear."

That's the way Henry was, always making you look inside for something...the fear...the courage...the light...the two-hundred-year-old Chinaman...

But still it went on, month after month of hysteria. And I guess you could say that we started disconnecting a little. We just didn't see any reason for it in Dogleg Bend, West Virginia. First it was bin Laden, then it was Saddam.

Sometime in the middle of all this, they started blasting the hell out of Spenser Mountain, like the mountain was to blame for 9/11.

ONE DAY DURING the spring of our sophomore year, well after our summer job had turned into a year-round arrangement, we were in the cabin—one fairly large room, divided informally into its parts: kitchen and living space spread out over three corners and Henry's bed in the fourth, across from the kitchen. In the center of the room stood a wood-burner. Dewey was pulling books from the shelves by Henry's bed. "What's with all the UFO books, Henry? You believe in little green men?"

It was true: a whole shelf lined with titles like *Aliens Among Us*, *Are UFO's Real?*, *The UFO Conspiracy*, and *Chariots of the Gods*. They were all paperbacks from the sixties or seventies, all similarly cheesy looking. On another shelf were hardbacks on the history of World War II and World War II aviation.

Even when Dewey was making fun, there was affection in it. Henry started chuckling.

"Aya, I dunno."

He showed us pictures from the books, animals etched into the Earth that could only be seen from the air. Dewey called them the NASCAR lines and we all laughed. Dewey had a name for nearly everything Henry told us about that afternoon, like the Doggone Tribe, some tribe in Africa who said they talked to the space brothers. He pulled out a World War II history book and showed us a passage that described balls of light that followed American bombers who called them foo fighters. It was pretty cool to find out where the band got its name. He even told us a story about a man who was given pancakes by aliens that landed in his backyard.

"So, you tell me, boys," he said. "Somethin's going on, but I don't know what it is." He pointed to the side of his head with a slightly curled finger. "Maybe it's all just going on in here, eh?"

"Or here," said Dewey, indicating his ass.

Henry stood up and patted him on the shoulder like a dog that you just don't know what to do with.

It was obvious that Henry did not disapprove of our partying as long as we didn't abuse his trust. Dewey had a girlfriend at this point and we both, with the optimism of the extremely horny, needed a place where we could get down to business if the situation ever arose. So, when Henry gave us permission to fix up his trailer for "entertaining," we got up in there and rearranged all the artwork so we could set up the bed in the living room. There really was no other room that would fit all the paintings. Then Dewey, in a stroke of genius, hung our favorite Old Stinky Joe painting on the wall in front of the bed. The "Love Shack" was born. Over the next few years, quite a few girls would look up at that painting and then snuggle in closer.

BY OUR JUNIOR year, Dewey had managed to save up enough money to get himself a used car from Rooster. It was a silver 1994 Honda Civic. It had been wrecked and the passenger door had been replaced with one painted orange.

Ugly as the thing was, Dewey loved it. The first day he had it, he picked me up and we cruised all over. I didn't think anything of it when he started up Morgan Hollow Road. I figured we were heading up to Kevin's Way, maybe to our friend Charlie's house. But when he stopped at the T-intersection at the top of Morgan Hollow and turned the car around, pointing it downhill, I knew what he was about to do.

Morgan Hollow Road, while not completely straight, only has one significant turn. Other than that, it is just very steep, leveling out briefly a couple times, where roads shoot off to either side. Before I could say anything, he smiled at me, put the car in neutral and let off the brake. As we began to roll forward, I said, "No."

"Yes." Dewey turned his attention to the road, gripped the wheel with both hands, and briefly raised his elbows as if they were wings. I don't remember everything I said as the car gained speed; probably "No" several times. I seem to remember saying, "You just got this car!" Mostly, I remember how my legs were locked, pressed into the footwell, my hands on the dash as if they could keep the engine from crushing me. Oh, and Dewey's grin.

And then we dropped onto the level spot. My stomach dropped out from under me, and we were airborne, Dewey yelling, "Woooooooo!" and me trying not to shit my pants. I don't think we were in the air long, even though it seemed like forever, and how would I have known? As we landed, I was already thinking about the next one. Luckily, he didn't shoot us out onto Route Twelve and into a coal truck, which was what I was envisioning during the second landing. If I would have had the ability to think at that moment, I might have been impressed that the car was still in one piece.

Dewey pulled off the road at the bottom. His shoulders slowly eased back onto his body. "We survived," he said with a satisfied sigh.

"The day is young," I replied, trying to relax my shaking legs.

"Oh, come on Ned. You know what Henry says about how you gotta find the things you're afraid of."

"I don't think that's what he had in mind." I was pissed. Aside from the stuff with Casey, this was the only other time that I was ever truly mad at Dewey.

WITH WHEELS, WE started looking for new places to party. That's how we ended up on Stiller Road out by the Spenser Mountain coal operation. We didn't figure there would be any traffic since everyone had sold out and moved away.

That evening, three carloads of us found a little field that everyone could pull into, got a fire going, and broke out a couple cases of beer. Later, Dewey stumbled into the woods to piss and came bursting out with the words, "Hey, come see!" Off we trotted after him, beers aloft, cigarettes lit, into the dark woods like Grimm's children.

The patch of forest wasn't much wider than the one we used to play in when we were five and it ended at a ten-foot chain-link fence with razor-wire strung along the top. On the other side of the fence, flat dead terrain spread out as far as we could see. This was where the strip mining had started, long since abandoned and dead.

"Look here." Dewey kicked one of the posts and it swayed like a dandelion in a stiff wind. "Three of 'em are like that," he said. "There must be rock underneath here and somebody didn't want to fuck with it."

So we did what any red-blooded, beer-drinking, high school boys would do. We stomped that fucking fence over and went for a walk on the moon.

We walked along the fence line, past some sort of depot that contained idle machines, until we could see the night operations lit in the distance. A couple of the guys turned back, but me, Dewey, and Charlie were just drunk enough to want to get closer. Staying concealed in the shadowy tree line, we were climbing now, and to our right, the surface of the Earth was beginning to recede. And then, we were at the top, our backs to the fence, and ten feet in front of us, the Earth ended. Stretched below, the terraces of giant Incans, long, looping roads, and massive machinery, Tonka-sized from here. Dust floated everywhere below us, a swirling brown mass with a life of its own. In the air, the distant sounds of beeping, scraping, and dumping gave color to the dull roar of the engines. It was a powerful sight that made us feel powerful, and we sat there smoking a blunt just a few feet from the two-hundred foot drop off. Three ships about to sail off the edge of the world.

III

ONCE, WHEN DEWEY was out with Allison Miller, I spent the day at Henry's looking at his books and asked him what World War II was like.

For two hours, my jaw hung open as he told me about being shot down, captured by the Japanese, and sent to the prison camp where he had to work the coal mine and eat maggots. Then, his escape when the monk helped him get out of Japan and into China. He got downright emotional during parts of it.

"I tell ya, Ned," he said when he was finished. "It all makes you appreciate the little gifts that the universe gives you." He was looking at me intensely and, for a brief moment, I heard my father's voice asking if the old man was a "prevert." I'm heartily ashamed of that thought, but no one had ever really looked at me like that before, with that kind of openness, that kind of love.

"You are a gift to me, Ned. You're one of the ways the universe has made it all alright."

And then, he told me one of those things that I'm still not sure I understand.

EVEN THOUGH DEBORAH didn't know it, Rooster was now our weed connection. One day, me and Dewey went out to Rooster's for a bag and found him sitting on his front porch. He wore jeans and a sleeveless Metallica t-shirt. He hadn't shaved in a few days.

"Super Dewey and the Ned-Man!" he said as we got out of the car and approached the porch. Rooster wasn't generally that friendly with us, so that greeting set us back on our heels, like small mammals suddenly wondering if there were hawks about.

"What's up, Rooster?" asked Dewey.

"Ah, shit, man, I don't know." His eyes darted to and fro, and his tight smile threatening to jump from his lips and dance a victory dance. He gestured to his surroundings. "What isn't up, you know? What isn't up? I ask you."

We held a healthy fear of Rooster's biker nature. We'd heard stories, so his behavior was disconcerting, and I was hardly surprised to hear Dewey forcing out a laugh.

"Man, yer in a good mood today, dawg."

"That I am, young Dewey." His smile left his head and floated around us like the Cheshire Cat, examining, wondering. The air was thick with potential energy that felt like it could go either way, good or bad.

"Say Rooster, ya suppose we could snag a little weed?"

He looked at us like he'd just remembered we were there.

"Sure," he said. "Wait here." He walked into his house like a man who knew exactly what he was doing, without asking us how much we wanted, or how much money we had. After fifteen minutes, we sat down on the edge of the porch.

Rooster emerged from the door much more tentatively than he had entered, looking like he was trying to remember something. He tossed a baggie to Dewey.

"What do I owe ya?"

"Ah fuck, I dunno Dewey. Couldn't get the fuckin scales to work right. Just gimme ten dollars."

Me and Dewey looked at each other like men who had stumbled onto a treasure but suspected a trap.

"You sure, man?" said Dewey. "Looks like more than that here."

"Yeah, fuck, I'm sure," said Rooster. "I tell you what. Make it twenty and I got something else here for you in my pocket."

"What is it?"

"That's a surprise." His eyebrows raised, and his smile once again floated about.

"We don't do the hard stuff, Rooster."

"I know it. I know it. This ain't like smack. Your mom'd kill me."

"Well, what is it?"

"Something every true-blooded young American superhero redneck has to try at least once. Now go on!" He held out his hand. "Super Dewey and the Ned-Man!"

He had us laughing along with his disembodied smile. Dewey pulled a twenty out and put it in Rooster's hand.

Rooster held out another baggie. "Have fun."

Dewey stuck the bag in his pocket without looking at it. We both said thanks and headed for the car. As we pulled out, I waved at Rooster, sitting on the porch. His smile waved back from the branches of a nearby oak tree.

WHEN WE UNROLLED our mystery-bag later, we found it filled with long twisted mushrooms with brown caps and bluish-gray stems.

"Magic mushrooms," said Dewey, marveling at the baggie hanging from his hands. This was a first for us. Dewey's face lit up with an idea. "Magic mushrooms on the moooooon!"

That night, we drove out to the field on Stiller Road, chewed up the foul-tasting things, and washed them down with a few Milwaukee's Bests.

It was dark on our trek through the woods, but moon parties had become a high school tradition, and we'd walked it many times. Soon, the woods thinned, and we came to where the chain-link fence was pushed over.

Those shrooms must have been gathering steam as we walked, because as soon as that vista opened before us, it was like we both exploded. Looking at that flat expanse laid out in front of me, I was overcome with the urge to run across it and took off, full blast, sprinting as fast as I could, feeling the power of it, the joy of it. I flew across the moon, a god among men. I was strong. I was alive. I had never felt this good my entire life.

I ran and ran and then just as quickly stopped and plopped down onto the ground, the mood gone. Dewey came running up behind me, grinning. "I almost lost ya. When did you get that fast?"

"I can do anything." I kind of believed it.

"Shit man, I hear ya. This is crazy cool."

Dewey walked out a few yards farther, and for a few moments, it was quiet.

Finally, Dewey said, "Ned, come here and look at this."

I rose and walked over, looking down into a crevasse, hard to tell how deep in the dark. But, deep.

"How'd you know to stop? You could have gone over."

"I didn't know."

Dewey started hopping up and down like he just didn't know what else to do, saying "Holy shit! Fuck fuck *fuck*, that's so cool! You *are* a superhero man! You got the super speed *and* the X-ray vision! You da man, Ned. You da Ned-man!"

I again sank to the ground, this time a little less godlike. If I'd run another twenty feet, I'd have broken my neck in the dark. The questions danced in the air around us, making the atmosphere heavier somehow, pressing us down into silence. And lo and behold, that silence began to grow.

Funny thing about mushrooms. They make you feel connected. They make you feel *more*, more even than you thought you could, and now the silence of the place had turned into a phantom, lurking in the dark, just out of sight. No crickets, no frogs out here. No plants except the occasional airborne weed. Nothing above the ground. Nothing below the ground. Even the earthworms were gone. For the first time, we experienced the moon as it really was: desolate, stripped, beaten. The crevasse in front of me was graphic proof that we were sitting upon the shattered Earth. There was nothing here but ghosts. I sat motionless as the lifelessness pressed in around me. I felt the horror of the universe. I wanted to leave but couldn't stand for fear of disturbing it and attracting the utter finality of the cosmos.

"I don't think I want to be here," said Dewey.

"Me neither."

Dewey stood up and started walking back and I followed him. The silence followed us, insistent, dead. It wasn't long before I snapped and began to run again, desperate to get out of there. We hit the wood line gasping for breath. I rolled onto the ground and stretched my hands out to the sides, laying them in the cool, damp leaf mold.

"Something's wrong there," Dewey kept saying, over and over. "Something's wrong."

"Let's get outta here," I said, but didn't move.

"I've been out there a million times," he said, looking back over his shoulder. "How could I have not known?"

Dewey dropped down to his knees and started touching the plants. "I remember now," he said. "I remember when we were kids."

I got up off the ground.

Dewey didn't say anything on the drive, but I could tell he was getting more and more mad. Of the two of us, he always had been the quicker to temper, but this was different. A switch had flipped inside him. I knew, because it had flipped in me too.

HENRY'S LIGHTS WERE off when we pulled up, so we just slipped quietly through the backyard and out to the field where we had a fire pit. We started a fire without speaking. It was as though we needed to suck in as much of the sounds of the night as we could, and any talk would get in the way. Henry's wind machine clinked and tinkled behind us.

Dewey broke in first. "I really can't believe I ain't never seen that before, Ned. It ain't right."

"I felt like I was in the middle of some big, black hole, and it was going to swallow me up."

"It was just empty, man. It ain't right."

"I feel better now."

"Yeah." Dewey let out a long breath. "Better. Here."

"Oh, what a sight. Men who've gazed on the darkness."

Henry came out of nowhere, slid right into the scene without hardly disturbing the universe at all, including us. Remarkable, considering our state of mind.

"Fuck the darkness," said Dewey.

"Aya, there ya go, Dewey," Henry said. "The darkness can't really touch ya when you got the righteous fire."

"We were out on the moon," I said.

Henry sat down and scrutinized us pretty closely. He must have known.

"It looks like you didn't have so much fun this time."

"Empty," said Dewey.

"Aya, not much life on the moon, and plenty of darkness, I'll warrant. A full half of it, if I remember correctly."

The fire spit from the damp wood. The sound of frogs carried on the breeze that rustled the tall grass in the field and the leaves of the trees.

"Our lives are being run by suicidal gods," said Dewey.

Henry stood up.

"Aya, it might seem that way," he said, "but it ain't the truth. Them pitiful gods only think they run things."

We kept looking at the fire.

Henry turned around, saying, "You're smart men." As the darkness shrouded his shoulders, he said, "You'll figure it out." A moment later, his voice emerged from the shadows again. "We all do," and then, more distant, "eventually."

We turned inward to our racing thoughts, both of us on our back looking at the stars, for the first time aware that we were hurtling into those cold depths, aware of everything around us at a level we'd never known before that night. Dewey was breathing long and deep, as if he were trying to pull the very life from the night.

"I did not know how empty was my soul until it was filled."

Dewey didn't talk like that. He was quoting some movie. He had a way of pulling film quotes out of his ass at the right time. I didn't know what movie it came from.

"You hear that frog?"

"There's only about a million frogs croaking, Dewey."

"Just that one. You hear it?

"Which *one?*"

"The one asking the question."

I listened and he was right. One, *just one*, of the croaks ended on an upward note. It sounded like he was stuck in a perpetual question that he asked over and over.

"I wonder what he's asking," said Dewey.

"I dunno, but it sounds like all them other frogs keep telling him the answer."

"Must not be a very good answer."

WE HEARD ABOUT the mountaintop removal protest near halfway through our senior year. Hell, everyone in town knew it was coming up. There was going to be celebrities and everything: Jimmy Howell, Tricia Patterson, even Mary Lee Ray who grew up in Trevelton before becoming a big country star. Me and Dewey were curious about the whole thing. The added bonus of getting to see movie star Jimmy Howell arrested made it irresistible. That morning, we blew off school and headed south on Twelve, toward the Big Empty.

Chaos reigned at the site entrance. State and county cops ushered away spectators who parked on the opposite side of the road by the news trucks. In front of each truck a tripod stood with a camera, some idle and some filming. A few cameramen held their equipment on shoulder mounts. Well-dressed correspondents chatted, smoked cigarettes, and looked bored. Some stood in front of their cameras. A county cop walked up to us and told us to move along. Dewey drove past the cameras at a crawl.

"Bet we get on the news somewhere," he said.

At the end of the line of news trucks, Dewey looked in his rearview to see if any of the cops were watching and whipped the Civic off the road to the right, turning a hundred eighty degrees, and sliding in behind the news truck. Man, he abused that car's suspension. From there, we snuck behind the news trucks on foot, like secret agents, dashing across any open space.

Dewey climbed the ladder on the back of one of the trucks and I followed him. No sooner had we gotten on the roof when a bald guy in a headset jumped out of the back and said, "Hey you two, get down off of there!"

"We will," said Dewey.

"No, I mean now!" He grabbed his headset, said, "Shit!" and climbed back into the truck.

Dewey and I had the best seats in the house. From the top of the van, our view was unobstructed, and it was there I saw the most beautiful girl in the world. Obviously, two flannel-clad rednecks had no business on top of a news truck, and she appeared to get a kick out of it. She had long brown hair in a braid, a small, dainty face and hands, and a hippie dress. She woreglasses. She smiled at me.

I. Loved. Her. I never thought such shit was possible.

County cops busted some heads that day. They weren't impressed with the celebrities, and yes, we got to see Jimmy Howell and Tricia Patterson arrested, cameras whirring and flashing. Then, Mary Lee Ray was cuffed and hauled away too, but you could tell they were gentler with her. Spectators applauded when she walked out there and laid down, though how that many spectators managed to avoid being shuffled off by the counties, I'll never know.

One by one, those protestors stretched out on the dirt road, and one by one, they were hauled off in plastic restraints.

Then, it was the braided girl's turn, and she looked to see if I was watching. As they were pushing her head down and into the squad car, she smiled at me again. When I told Dewey about it afterward, he said, "Yeah, she was smiling at me."

As we climbed off the news van and got back in Dewey's car, he said, "Ya know, Ned, them people's hearts is in the right place, but they ain't never gonna stop nothin' like that."

THERE WAS NO way me or Dewey could have gone to college. There weren't any Promise Scholarships for us. I worked for a while at the convenience store after graduation, and Dewey managed to get a year in at Walmart before they fired him for misplacing six-packs out by the dumpster. Fortunately, Henry always had an odd job or two for us, and during those post-graduate days we hung out with him more than ever. Now that we were older, I barely stayed at home, unless it was Dewey's. Though I technically still lived there, I avoided King Jack of the double-wide.

By this time, we knew the coal company was after Henry's land. Shit, it seemed like they were after everyone's land. But they were especially greedy for Henry's parcel. I hadn't even known he owned that much of the mountain, but it was pretty hard not to notice all the coal reps stopping by week after week. Henry dispatched them with his usual flair and they always left frustrated after their logic met Henry's common sense.

We tried to stay out of the way at the beginning, but after a while, we could see it was wearing Henry down. Sure enough, we managed to get ourselves on the porch when the next of the company men showed up. We listened with

Henry as the man explained how it was in Henry's best interest, and how it was likely they'd be taking the whole other side of the mountain anyway, and how he didn't really want to live here when that was going on, and how he ought to be able to have some peace at this point in his life.

During the entire ultra-rational argument, Dewey never took his eyes off the guy. He was playing a part in a movie and he was good. When it was over, and the rep awaited Henry's response, his counterattack already on his lips, Dewey leaned over to Henry, never taking his eyes off the suit. "Henry," he said, "you want we should kill him for ya?"

Well, you never saw a guy get so uncomfortable so fast. He was gone within minutes after Henry said, "I don't think that'll be necessary, Dewey." Henry played it nicely, even though he didn't know it was coming. Ultimately, the coal rep visits became less frequent, and every time one came, the first thing they'd ask Henry was if his crazy grandkids were around.

It was all beginning to weigh on us: the mountaintop removal, the wars, the stupid people around town who were flipping out about Muslims and Democrats while the real enemy was just down the road, eating their lives, their history, their freedom, and their happiness like sweet, black candy.

One day, late that summer, we heard about the 9/11 five-year anniversary vigil scheduled for downtown.

"Are you fucking kiddin' me?" asked Dewey. "Do you really think any of these people give a shit about what happened five years ago? Or do you think they care more about what they look like in the paper with a candle in their hand and fakesad on their face? Bet it'll be a real 'kill the Arabs' good time."

That was it for Dewey. The town had become fake like the rest of America. Fake patriots. Fake political experts. Fake Christians. Fake sorrow.

"It's gotta end sometime, Ned, and I say we're the guys to end it."

So, on September 11th at 7 p.m., after downing a six-pack, I drove Dewey's car down Main Street in downtown Dogleg Bend with the stereo blasting "You Know What You Are?" by Nine Inch Nails, as loud as Dewey's pitiful speakers could handle, past seventy-five somber anniversary celebrants, police officers, and public officials…with Dewey's ass hanging out of the passenger window, framed in orange.

We had a jump on them, of course, and lost the Sheriff's Deputies by pulling into a secluded turnaround and waiting them out. Then, we hightailed it to Henry's so we could tell him we might not be up for a while. He kept us there for the night, so we missed seeing our senior pictures on the eleven o'clock news.

HENRY TOOK US to the Sheriff's office in Trevelton the next morning where we were met by J. Allan Davidson. Henry's attorney kept us out of jail and, by the next week, got us out of it with three-hundred-dollar fines.

The damage was done in Dogleg Bend, though. Me and Dewey were pariahs. People called us Arab-lovers. Apparently, any sentiment seen as "un-American" automatically qualified you as a terrorist sympathizer. Dewey's woman broke up with him. Pop threw me out of the house. He wanted to anyway and it didn't hardly make any difference. I just moved my stuff fifty yards to Dewey's place above the bar. Deborah didn't care, and honestly, I think she enjoyed tweaking my mom, who always treated her like dirt.

The "fag" comments got nastier. One night, Gil Wagner, with his wife and a couple of his friends, cornered us in front of the Wet Whistle, the only bar left in Dogleg Bend unless you counted The Henhouse. Gil was a long-time dick from grade school right on through.

"It's the two homos, fellas. These two been packing the fudge since way back."

They were blocking our way

"Fuck off, Gil," Dewey said, and Gil decked him.

"Come on," said his wife, rolling her eyes and tugging at his arm, but Gil wasn't moving.

"So, which one of ya is the woman?" he said. "I'll bet it's Foster, right? What do you do Burke, wait for him to bend over and pray to Mecca and then slip him the meat?"

They all left laughing. It was a short time after this incident that Dewey looked over at me and asked, "Ned, are we gay, you think?" Shaken up and feeling like outcasts, we needed to find out, even if we were pretty sure of the answer. Don't think it was easy, that kiss. It's never easy to think you might not be who you thought you were. And it was damn awkward to boot. In fact, from then on it became our personal joke for all awkward moments. "That was almost as bad as kissing Ned Foster."

Still, it got under our skins, all that Arab-homo-crap, Dewey more than me. All his life, he'd had to put up with the stigma of being the "stripper's kid." A few nights later, standing in line in Walmart with a twelve-pack, the two old ladies in line behind us started having a conversation about how the world sure was going to hell in a handbasket when you had to wait in line behind a Muslim and the perverted offspring of strippers. Dewey was fuming on the drive back from the store and whipped the car into a cemetery, jumped out, and started kicking over tombstones.

"Fuck!" Kick. "All!" Kick. "You!" Kick. "Mother!" Kick. "Fuckers!" Kick.

It was just bad luck that at that moment a Sheriff's car pulled in behind us. When the deputy saw who it was standing among the horizontal tombstones, he said, "Well, well." They weren't fond of the two of us, either. Of course, J. Allan Davidson was able to get him out with a fine and some community service cleaning cemeteries, but not before Dewey spent the night in county lock-up. He was way too quiet when I picked him up and I could see it hurt him to move. He wouldn't talk to me about that night, ever. He swore to me that he would never go to jail again.

It felt like there was something we needed to do but we didn't know what it was yet. It took a couple years of pranking the denizens of Dogleg Bend to understand that it was all missing something. But when we finally took an honest look, we understood what truly made us feel hopeless and small and angry.

LIKE AMERICA, WE made our last trip to the moon, our spacesuits blacker than our painted faces, our oxygen packs replaced with backpacks containing five bags of sugar, our steps the long, slow, bounding steps of moonwalkers in half-gravity.

The equipment depot had moved farther in since we'd been here last. The whole area where we used to party looked exactly the same. It was dead. It would be dead for a long time, and now the destruction stretched a lot further. It took us a half hour to find the depot, still out on the fringes of the operation, unlit. Dewey pulled the wire-cutters from his pack, chopped a line down the chain-link, and we slipped through it like seasoned burglars. We didn't know if any of those gargantuan machines were being used anymore, but we sugared every fuel tank we could figure out how to open, including a few company pickups. When we were done, Dewey pulled a can of spray-paint out of his pack and wrote "Friends of Coal" on the side of one of the pickups.

Then, we hightailed it to the car and drove further out Stiller Road until we came to one of the abandoned farms sold to the coal company. We pulled around the back of the barn and took off all our clothes, wiping the shoe polish off our faces with rags. Then, we took the clothes, the backpacks, the sugar bags and the spray-paint can and put them in a hole we'd dug earlier. Dewey dumped an entire can of lighter fluid on the pile, threw in the can, and lit it. After it burned down a little, which didn't take long, I started filling in the hole again while Dewey took the wire-cutters into the barn and hung them on a hook in a corner beneath some stairs, like a forgotten tool. We dressed and drove back toward town and the Wet Whistle as quickly as we could, hoping we could make it look like we'd been there all night.

THE NEXT TWO weeks, we hung out exclusively at the Henhouse apartment and made sure that people knew we were there. We didn't want to draw unwanted attention to Henry, so we stayed away from him. I felt pretty bad about that. But we were men on the edge, wondering if this person or that was following us with their eyes, wondering how long that car had been parked out front.

"Jesus Christ," said Dewey about a week into it. "This sucks."

Nevertheless, no one called to tell us about cops asking questions. No strangers were actually following us with their eyes and there were no strange cars outside except for the horny guys from Trevelton who came down here to the strip bar so their wives wouldn't find out. After another week of this, Dewey could take no more.

"If I'm going to get caught, then I'm going to get caught having fun, not sitting here, holed up like Saddam."

I was tired of it, too. We needed to get out under the stars. Since we couldn't go to Henry's field, we went further out our road, back to where we used to camp by Diggers Creek, where we used to hunt crawdads, minnows, and salamanders. The salamander days were over for Diggers Creek and we could feel that too, quietly drinking our beers in the dark with the bubbling water speaking of hope.

"Boy, you can't go back, can ya?" Dewey finally said.

There was no comfort here.

When we finished our beers, we got back in Dewey's car to head home. We didn't get a mile down the road before the Sheriff's patrol passed us going the other way and put on their lights, turning around to come after us. Dewey floored it.

"I AIN'T GOIN back to jail," he said as we flew down the road of our childhood, the cops never more than a turn behind us.

"They're on us, Dewey! What the hell are we gonna do?"

"Better put your seatbelt on."

"Shit." I reached for the belt. I knew what he had in mind. It's funny how, when you've been close to someone a long time, you can almost read his mind.

As we got close to our parent's places, Dewey did what I figured. He turned off the headlights and slammed through the barbed wire fence on the side of the road, launching us from a four-foot embankment, down into the field where we used to chase garter snakes. Somehow, we stayed upright and kept bouncing across the field until the axle broke and the left front tire fell off. The car lurched to the left, grinding to a halt, throwing my head against the passenger window hard enough to make my ears roar.

Dewey dove out of the car, yelling, "We gotta split up!"

I jumped out but had to hold onto the car because of my spinning head. The cops apparently saw us fly into the field and pulled over, shining a spotlight down on the car.

"Where do we meet?"

"The field out behind the Smith place." He took off up the hill toward the trees. I stepped to follow, but my knees were giving out, shaking, my hand gripping the side mirror for support. A deputy charged across the field toward me like a pro linebacker. The rhythmic clank and shift of his utility belt bouncing up and down and the heavy thuds of his booted steps drew close behind me.

Some moments in life have a clarity that lasts forever, even when the surrounding time is lost, like the moment when Dewey and I first saw each other through the trees when we were four. The instant just before the gunshot will remain with me if I live to be a hundred years old.

I couldn't let go of the mirror. I couldn't run. I was done for and I knew it. Dewey must have sensed it, because he stopped at the edge of the woods and turned around. That's when it happened. For a split second, it all became Henry's painting that hung in the "Love Shack." Dewey was Old Stinky Joe, emerging from the edge of the forest.

And then, I was eating field grass. The deputy on top of me screamed, "Gun!" and a single pistol shot reverberated through the field and off the hills like a ghostly echo from the Civil War.

As the deputy escorted me to the car, I looked back to see Dewey lying in a heap, illuminated by spotlight.

The cop that shot him looked familiar.

He punched me in the stomach.

IV

THE TRIAL WAS interesting.

Of course, J. Allan Davidson was on the job at Henry's request.

"I don't know how much I'm going to be able to help you this time, Ned," he said at the beginning. "They've got security footage of you two sugaring those tanks. They've got store surveillance video from the Walmart showing you both buying the sugar. They lifted both your prints from the scene. They found your wire-cutters." He shook his head. "It should be a case of simple vandalism and property damage, but I'm telling you, Ned, there's big-time political pressure coming down on this. They're calling it environmental terrorism. Trying to bring the Feds in."

I didn't know what to say.

"I'm going to do my best for you. For whatever reason, Henry loves you and I've known Henry my whole life, since Dad was his attorney. But I think you've got a hard road ahead."

He was right.

The regional jail wasn't a good scene to begin with, but once they started calling me a terrorist on television, things got significantly worse. That's how I ended up in the infirmary with a detached retina and an eye patch.

Before the hearing dates, Henry visited as often as he could make the seventy-five-mile journey. A couple times, J. Allan Davidson drove him down when he just didn't have it in him. He was ninety-four, after all. I could tell it hurt him when he first saw my sorry state.

"Aw, Ned," he said, looking at my patched mug, that high, soft voice cracking.

"Yeah," I said.

Henry didn't say anything for a few minutes. Finally, he leaned over the table as far as he could and locked his gaze onto my good eye. I almost cried, looking at him like that.

"Ned." His voice had firmed into a tone I'd never heard from him. It was the tone of someone who had seen worse and survived. "This is important, you hear?"

I nodded.

"There's something you have to remember. The universe is beautiful, even in its pain. There are times when pain is a friend, reminding you that you are alive, that you've been given the gift of awareness, and that how you use that gift is up to you. You can sacrifice it and drown in your misfortune, or you can embrace this moment and come out of it a better man. Do you understand?"

I nodded again. And I understood.

J. ALLAN DAVIDSON managed to beat the federal charges that were brought against me in front of the grand jury. He painted a picture of two ornery boys who liked to pull pranks and successfully undermined any political intent in the grand jury's eyes. The state court was not as pleasant an experience.

J. Allan Davidson brought in witnesses from the Department of Highways to testify about our road sign prank. He displayed photographs of the liposuction billboard we defaced. He even called Mayor Bradley to testify about the yard gnome that kept moving to random parts of his yard. This elicited snickers from the courtroom and I had a hard time keeping a smile off my face, much to my attorney's consternation.

In the end, I was sentenced to three to five years in the regional jail for a variety of charges, among them, willful destruction of property (they said we did a million dollars in damage. I hope that's not an exaggeration) and creating a public nuisance.

As I was being escorted from the proceedings, I looked to the back of the courtroom and there she was, the girl from the protest. She smiled at me for the third time when our eyes met, only that time, it contained pity. A universe that can deal a bad hand can deal a good hand at the same time. That's what Henry was talking about.

Eventually, as it became clear that my eye had healed as much as it was going to, and my time in the safety of the infirmary was growing short, J. Allan Davidson again rode in on his white horse. Arguing that it was becoming more and more clear that I was not going to survive my incarceration given my undeserved reputation as a terrorist and general enemy of Our Holy Lady of Coal, he managed to get me transferred to a low security facility outside of Charleston.

They buried Dewey in Sunny Hills Cemetery.

THE LAST TIME Henry visited was a few weeks back.

"I don't know how many more times I'll be able to make this trip, Ned." This place was even farther away than the regional jail.

"That's okay Henry. I'm doing good and it's all because of you."

"I've missed ya, son. Been quiet up there on the mountain."

I could feel the loneliness coming off of him and felt horrible for being where I was.

"Henry, why did you ever move out there by yourself? Why'd you become a hermit?"

"Ah," he said, waving his hand in the air, "I was just sick of people back then. Didn't see any reason to be around 'em." He smiled. "Truth was, I was just all wrapped up in my own pain. Then I got out there for a while and I discovered something."

I waited, then asked, "What?"

"The wild places, Ned. Those places throb with more than just life, son. When you finally come to understand that sound, that silence, then you understand it for what it is. Awareness. I found out that the more I paid attention to it, and the more I looked inside for the truthful me, the more amazing and mysterious the world became. I wouldn't ever want to lose that experience, you know. I got no regrets." He examined his wrinkled hands, folded on the table. "But I always knew there was an empty space, too."

"And how did you fix that?"

"Well, I didn't. I had faith. I waited. And the universe fixed it for me."

"How?" There was a whole group of empty spaces floating around inside of me now for which I needed a solution.

"Well," he said, smiling, "I ran out of toilet paper."

It took me a second to cipher that out before I remembered and smiled back at him.

"And I've always wondered," I said. "Old Stinky Joe…"

"I spec you wonder why y'all never got to see him in all this time."

"Yeah." I grinned, like one who knows he's been willingly joshed.

"I always wondered that too, but Joe, he follows rules that I don't always understand. The rules of the old wild."

He trailed off a moment, as if following something in another place.

"Seems like maybe he just shows up for the folks that need him worst," he said. "Once, I thought it was going to happen, that he was going to show himself to someone besides me. I smelled him coming and everything. But the feller that was sitting there with me up and run off, and Joe never came out of the woods." His face took on a puzzled, scrunched expression. "You know, I always figured he was here for that other feller. That was just kinda disappointing, considering he hadn't ever introduced himself to you and Dewey. I told him so, too."

"And what did Joe say?"

Henry laughed, and it reminded me of all those years ago in the grocery store parking lot. He pushed himself up from the table. "He said, 'Tough shit, Billy Bob. Drink your tea.'"

"I love you, Henry."

"I love you too, son."

He patted me on the cheek. The guard didn't say anything.

"Maybe that's the sound of one hand clapping," he said as he walked away.

MY SISTER, JENNY, has been to see me a few times, too. She's married now. We don't have much in common, but it's been nice getting to know her.

"Pop's sick, you know," she said on the first visit. "Cirrhosis."

"You couldn't see that coming?"

"I think Ma would've been to see you, but he won't let her."

"I'm not gonna cry about that, either."

"I know."

She'd had her problems with them too. If I had to guess, I'd say she married just to get out of there. I hope that doesn't come around and bite her on the ass, but when I talked to her, she always seemed happy enough.

"When you get out, you come to my house on Thanksgiving, y'hear?"

I SAW J. Allan Davidson last week. He came to tell me that Henry was dead. The last piece of my world was gone.

As I sat there crying, he said, "I know you loved him, Ned. He loved you too. So, I'm hoping that what I tell you next will soften this blow a little." He waited for me to look at him. "Henry left his entire estate to you."

"What?"

"Four hundred acres up there on the mountain where his cabin is, another twenty down by the river, that stretch of land where the old mill sits, and everything contained on those properties."

"What?"

"There is also a considerable amount of liquid assets, including stocks and cash, all of which will be going into a trust until you are a free man again."

"What about his family? He always said they wanted his property so they could sell it."

"The family has already filed suit to challenge the will on the grounds that Henry was incompetent. But when Henry drew up the will, he anticipated that. He obtained three separate doctor reports attesting to his competence, which we notarized and had attached to the will itself. They don't stand a chance. You are a rich man. What do you think?" Davidson scrutinized me. I was looking off into the space between the molecules of the table. I could see Henry in there, waving, his broad smile totally concealed and yet totally exposed by the bushy white whiskers.

"Money don't mean shit. I learned that much from Henry."

"Henry didn't think too highly of money, I know."

"I'm just happy to get the cabin." I started crying again when I thought about walking around that place now. How was that going to feel without the people who made it special to begin with? Would it just be me and my pain, or would it fill my soul like it did Henry's?

"So, Ned," he said, "I guess my first question is this: Do you wish to continue retaining my services as a representative of the estate?"

The question was foreign to my ears and it took me a moment to process.

"Well…yeah, I guess I do."

"And are you comfortable enough with me to sign a Power of Attorney agreement, so I can manage the estate's daily upkeep until you are free?"

"Comfortable? I like you, J. Allan."

"Good. I like you too, Ned. And since I work for you now, why don't you call me John."

"Okay…John."

"He always told me you were the one, Ned. The guy who wouldn't ever sell his land to the coal company. Was he right?"

"I wouldn't sell those fuckers the snot from my nose."

John laughed and then appeared to collect himself. "Ned, I told you my daddy was Henry's lawyer and that we went way back. I was in 'Nam, you know. Saw some pretty terrible things, and when I got back, I was in bad shape. Dad sent me up to talk to Henry, and Henry told me about his experience in World War Two. Did you know he tried to pull one of his buddies from a burning plane? His friend was on fire too, already dead. Did you know that? I loved the guy for that, for sharing that with me, and for listening to my stories, and offering that kooky advice of his—the inner light, and all that…I had tremendous respect for the man. So, I have to know, Ned. Why you? What made him think you were the one?"

"He told me, once, that I was someone he used to know."

"Yeah, that sounds like him. You believe it?"

"Right now, I don't know what to believe."

"I figure," he said, and then, after falling into the pose of deep thought, he rose out of it with the very face of recognition. "Holy crap," he said. "Ricky. Old Ricky, the monk who helped him escape! Is that it?"

I nodded.

"Well, I'll be damned." He gave me a look of appraisal. "So, what of it, bud? You got an old Buddhist monk floating around in there?" He moved his head from side to side as if he were trying to peek behind my eyes.

I laughed, finally. "I dunno, man. It's a mystery to me."

"And what I'm about to tell you may make it all the more inscrutable, Ned. You see, we drafted that will in 1997."

"What?" It took me a second. "But I didn't start working for him till…"

"I know. You see? How did he know?"

THE CELL IN this facility is more like a one-room apartment with iron bars. The window opens a few inches, allowing the wind to bring me news. Among the stories wafting through was one about Bergen County Deputy Sheriff Thomas Price, the cop acquitted of Dewey's shooting. He came up missing some time back. No one knows what happened to him. I have my suspicions.

I wish I knew what to say about Dewey that didn't sound stupid, something other than, "Deep down, he was a good guy," or, "He was misunderstood." All I know is I loved his flawed heart.

Henry? What can I say there? I don't know about all those stories he told us. Sometimes, I wanted to pretend it was all just the poetry of a gentle loony. But those were some of the most honest stories, I think, no matter how ridiculous they were. They float around me still, every night, borne on the breeze.

Last night, the draught through the window carried a foul stench, strong and persistent, and I had trouble falling asleep. I thought it might be another chemical spill in Charleston and lay here imagining bottled water and no showers for another six months. I must have become accustomed to the stink eventually, because I fell asleep and had a dream.

Me and Dewey were driving down the road, at night, and hit the big straight stretch south out of town. There's not too many straight stretches around Dogleg Bend, but that one goes on for a while, rising up and down, and we were flying out that road, this time rocking to "Stand Up" by The Prodigy. In the dream, me and Dewey were who we are now, right now; I was even wearing my eye patch. And when we raised our beers and Dewey said, "It's all good, Ned," we were looking at each other with the knowledge of everything that had happened. It felt like the past, the present, and the future were all wrapped up together.

Out in front of us, lightning struck the Earth and a toad fell out of the sky onto the pavement. Dewey accelerated, squashing the thing flat as a pancake. We hit the crest of the hill that opens onto the devastation of Spenser Mountain at what must have been a hundred miles an hour. At the top, we shed the chains of gravity, the car launching into the air, and as we flew past that lunar landscape, we both raised our middle fingers high. Super Dewey and the Ned-Man. The wind was swirling through the car, and out on the night, we could hear the mournful wails of Old Stinky Joe echoing through that new, dead valley, crying, "This was Henry Harper! This was my friend!"

Then, the destruction was gone, a victim of its own concept, and we sailed across the stars in a silver Honda Civic with an orange door, the moon behind us, waiting to be reborn.

About the Author

C.M. CHAPMAN began writing fiction in the mid 80's as an undergrad at West Virginia University. After a 25-year hiatus during which he did creative work for WCLG Radio in Morgantown, he returned to writing in 2012. He has appeared in numerous journals, including *Cheat River Review, Limestone, Still: The Journal, Unlikely Stories, Dark Mountain* in the U.K., and the anthology, *So It Goes: A Tribute to Kurt Vonnegut.* He is the author of the chapbook, *Music & Blood,* from Latham House Press, and is currently working on several new projects. He is a graduate of the low-residency MFA program at West Virginia Wesleyan College, where he has served as The McKinney Teaching Fellow and adjunct professor of English.

About the Press

UNSOLICITED PRESS IS a small press in Portland, Oregon. The team, made up of volunteers, works feverishly hard to publish fiction, poetry, and creative nonfiction. Every book is a piece of art, a true labor of love.

Learn more at unsolicitedpress.com